ARABIAN COLLUSION

A NOVEL

JAMES LAWRENCE

Cover and book layout by www.ebooklaunch.com

Dedication

This book is dedicated to my wife and family.
Without their support and assistance, it would not have been possible
to complete this book.

About the Author

James Lawrence has been a soldier, small business owner, military advisor, and international arms dealer. He is the author of four novels in the Pat Walsh series, Arabian Deception, Arabian Vengeance, Arabian Fury and Arabian Collusion.

CHAPTER 1

Riyadh, Saudi Arabia

Prince Turki bin Talal Abdulaziz tried to sit up in an attempt to get out of bed. A bout of dizziness forced his head back down onto the pillow. He was in a king-sized bed in a suite located on the third floor of the Riyadh Ritz Carlton. The surroundings were opulent, the bed soft, expansive and luxurious. The grandeur did nothing to salve the pain shooting through every muscle in his body, especially the throbbing agony in his back. He reached over to the nightstand and grabbed a half-liter-sized plastic Evian water bottle. Unsteadily, he twisted off the cap and with trembling hands brought the bottle to his lips. It took several tries, but eventually, he was able to splash enough fluid into his mouth to quench his thirst before slipping back into unconsciousness.

When Prince Turki awoke, it was morning; he could tell from the sliver of sun brightening the room through the narrow gap in the heavy curtains. The sheets around his waist were moist. He had either wet himself again, or it was the night sweats brought on by his nightmares; he couldn't tell, and he didn't care. Too tired and in too much pain to get up and clean himself, he lay still, helpless, staring at the ceiling, listening for the sound he had dreaded every morning for the past week.

As if on cue, he heard the sound of footsteps approaching his door. His heartbeat went into overdrive. The footsteps triggered another panic attack, and he was struggling to breathe by the time he heard the door open. Then came the familiar South African baritone.

"Wakey, wakey, princeling; time for another meeting with Mr. Van Doren."

1

Strong hands clamped down on his ankles and he was dragged off the foot of the bed. His back and head thudded against the hardwood floor. He slid easily across the polished wooden bedroom floor and then, with less ease, across the tile of the living room. Eventually, he felt the friction burn of the thick corridor carpet abrading his naked back. The trip ended when he was dragged by his heels into a hotel room at the end of the corridor. Once inside the makeshift interrogation room, his bony naked body was lifted by strong hands and he was strapped down to a wooden chair. His feet were shoved into a plastic tub of water. He felt alligator clips bite into his scrotum and a pail of cold water was splashed across his face and chest. After what felt like an eternity filled with dread and fear, a short red-headed man entered his field of view.

"I had a meeting with your cousin last night after you retired to your room. I proposed your offer of fifty-three billion dollars. I conveyed your promise of no retribution and your assurance that fifty-three billion is the maximum amount of liquidity you have. I was very persuasive in making your case. Unfortunately, your cousin is a very stubborn man. He's convinced seventy-five billion is achievable; he believes I just haven't provided you with the proper motivation." Van Doren nodded his head. A rubber dog bone was shoved into the Prince's mouth. He heard the metallic click of the switch being thrown and then felt the lightning strike. A surge of electricity convulsed every muscle in his body and then a red flash blanketed his vision. He regained consciousness to the familiar copper taste in his mouth and the smell of ozone in the air. Unsure how long he'd been out, he did his best to convince his captors he was still unconscious.

A bucket of ice-cold water caused him to betray his deception. "Your cousin thought it would help if you met with some of the family members who refused his generous offer of restitution. Only the most compassionate of leaders would allow criminals like you to return the money stolen from the Saudi Arabian people to pay for your corruption." The Prince felt himself being unstrapped and dragged from the chair. Naked and wet, he was dragged on his back along the corridor, into an elevator, down several stories and then through a kitchen. He heard a metal latch open and the sound of a vacuum seal being broken. He saw a thick, heavily insulated steel door, and he instantly felt a biting cold. He knew immediately he'd been dragged into a freezer. Lying on his back, looking at the ceiling, he folded his arms across his wet chest and began to shiver. He turned to his left and saw racks of frozen food. With what little strength he still possessed, he turned his head to the right. The sight shocked him. The wall was lined with bodies. He counted seven. He recognized all of them. His second cousin, Major General Hussain Ali, was the first in the line, his features frozen in a scream. Ice crystals had formed in his eyes and hair, making for an eerily grotesque sight. The other six cadavers were frozen in similar states of ante-mortem distress. All appeared to have died in the throes of agony. He screamed.

When he awoke, he once again found himself strapped to the chair, with his feet in the familiar water bucket. The hard pinch of the alligator clips against his badly bruised genitals focused his attention. He felt the water splash against his body and prepared himself for what was to come.

"Your cousin has agreed to come down to seventy billion. This is his last offer, you can either accept it or go into the deep freeze permanently. What's it going to be?" snarled Van Doren.

A feeling of even deeper despair fell over the Prince. He knew if he agreed to seventy billion his life would be spared for the moment, but the reprieve would be short-lived. He would never be able to come up with the money and once the Crown Prince learned he couldn't pay, he would be killed in an even worse way. He simply didn't have seventy billion in liquid assets. Although his net worth as reported by Forbes Magazine was well over one hundred billion, most of those assets were not easily transferable and if he tried to liquidate quickly, the sale would depress the asset price and he would be lucky to get even half. He started to sob uncontrollably. He heard the metallic click of the switch being thrown and then the lights went out.

The next morning, the Prince awoke in a different room. He was clothed in silk pajamas. He felt a heavy object around his right ankle. He reached down to remove it but found it was locked. An Indian servant entered the room and rolled a breakfast service of coffee, juices, fruits, and meats to the lounge chair next to the window. It took all of his energy, but the Prince crawled out of bed and seated himself for his first real meal in weeks. He was starving. He had no idea how much weight he had lost during his ordeal, but if the flesh hanging from his arms and legs were any indication, it had been a lot.

Hours later, Van Doren walked into the room, unannounced, as if he owned it. With him was a tall, middle-aged Saudi Arabian citizen wearing the local dress—a white kandura and red-and-white checkered keffiyeh. The Prince didn't recognize the man.

"The Crown Prince has generously decided to accept your offer of fifty-three billion. He is both kind and compassionate. He asked me to inform you that future corruption will not be dealt with as leniently. These are desperate times, and because of the serious financial crisis Saudi is facing, for the good of the Country he is willing to accept your offer of restitution instead of the retribution you deserve," Van Doren said.

"Talal is here to work out the details with you and your lawyers. You'll not be permitted to leave the hotel grounds until you've fulfilled your end of the bargain. That ankle bracelet you're wearing has an explosive charge inside it. It works like an invisible leash for a dog; if you try to exit the grounds it will detonate, and you'll lose your foot. We also have a guard force monitoring your movements from the signal given off by the bracelet. If you try to escape, you can be sure we'll drag what's left of you into the deep freeze."

Over the next ten weeks, the Prince had his business managers and lawyers generate the documents that allowed him to sign away fifty-three billion dollars from his vast empire to the government of Saudi Arabia. He didn't see Van Doren again, although the memory of his nemesis was rarely out of his mind. The hotel was swarming with his cohorts wearing the same distinctive black Frontier Security polo shirts as worn by Van Doren. When he was finally released from the hotel, his first act was to lease a private jet, as his Boeing 757 had just been sold, and fly to London. His second act was to plot his revenge.

CHAPTER 2

Homs, Syria

Sara strained to find the tail lights of the Toyota Land Cruiser they were following through the thick dust. In the dawn light, the cloud of dust particles had an orange hue that gave the surrounding scenery a sepia-like quality.

"How much further, Saed?" she asked the driver.

"We're almost there Doctor, another twenty, maybe thirty minutes."

Sara shifted her gaze to Saed. He was a heavy-set man in his late thirties, a pleasant laid-back guy, with a ready smile. Saed worked for Shirin International as a combination driver, interpreter, and security provider. Sara was happy for the security; they were driving north from the Syrian city of Homs, through the Idlib Governorate, the last area of Syria still not returned to the full control of the Assad regime.

Sara Salam's official title was Assistant Director of Middle Eastern Antiquities at the University of Pennsylvania Cultural Heritage Center. She was part of a cooperative effort between UPCHC and Shirin International to save the antiquities that were regularly being stolen and ravaged because of the Syrian Civil War.

As the sun rose higher in the morning sky, visibility improved. Eventually, Sara was able to make out a cluster of buildings on the horizon. Above the village on a hill, she could see the stone ruins that marked their destination. The village of Deir Semaan is home to a large Byzantine-era monastery. Prior to the war, it had a population of five thousand, although now it's mostly deserted. In 400 A.D., St. Simeon Stylites, a fifth-century monk, set off a trend among his fellow hermits by living on top of a pillar. St. Simeon climbed a pillar inside the church in 412 A.D. in order to get away from a horde of disciples and onlookers who pursued him after being drawn by stories of his lifestyle of extreme self-denial. St. Simeon once survived the forty days of Lent without eating or drinking anything, an achievement he followed up by standing stock still until he collapsed. Because of his growing popularity, in order to escape the growing masses of followers, he spent the remainder of his life on a succession of ever-higher pillars. After he died, his fame grew even more, and spawned scores of imitators, known as Stylites from the Greek word for pillar, "style."

The monastery, northwest of Aleppo, has been a tourist attraction for centuries, and has come under the control of different groups during the course of the civil war, including the Free Syrian Army, Islamic State of Iraq and the Levant (ISIL), the Kurdish YPG, the Islamist Group Ahar al-Sham, as well as the Turkish Army. It remains close to the front line between rebels, including Jabhat al-Nusra, the local al-Qaeda branch, the Kurdish forces from the YPG, and the Assad regime forces. Located in the Arfin valley, forty miles north of Aleppo, the area is of strategic importance to the Turkish, Syrian, and Kurdish people. Value is never a good thing in a war because it always invites more fighting. In May 2016, Russian bombers weighed in on the conflict and destroyed St. Simeon's pillar and parts of the monastery.

Sara's convoy passed through the battle-scarred village and climbed the winding road up the hill. They halted in front of the ruins of the monastery. Sara stepped out of her vehicle and joined the others who were assembling around the hood of the lead vehicle. She greeted Doctor Wolfgang Boetter and Doctor Felix Reddinger. Wolfgang was a German in his sixties. Tall and thin, decked out in a safari hat and khaki expedition clothing, the genial Bavarian greeted Sara with a smile. Felix was a Swiss citizen in his late thirties. An academic and outdoor enthusiast who was raised in Africa, Felix was armed with both a pistol and a menacing-looking black HK416 carbine. Unlike the affable Wolfgang, Felix wore a serious demeanor.

Wolfgang poured coffee from a silver thermos as they waited for the other two members of the inspection team to join them. Sara sipped the strong, steaming liquid and nodded to Wolfgang in appreciation. Doctor Wolfgang produced a box of chocolates and offered her the open box. Sara studied the assortment and selected a square and then turned to greet the rest of the group. Ole was a Norwegian, former military, and still looked the part of a special forces' operator. Ole, like Felix, wore tactical clothing and came armed. Ole was in his early forties; he was a wealthy man who started out as a donor to Shirin before taking a more active role in preventing the looting and destruction of Syrian history. Adolpho was an Italian, a dapper fifty-year-old professor from the University of Rome. Unlike the others, who were dressed for the field, he wore a navy-blue blazer and shiny Italian leather loafers.

As soon as the five academics and four drivers were assembled, Doctor Wolfgang addressed the group.

"Two days ago, we received a report of looting at the St. Simeon Cathedral. Our task today is to catalog the damage. Because it's not safe to remain here overnight, our time on site will be limited. We'll depart no later than four this afternoon in order to make it back to our compound before it gets dark. That leaves us only seven hours to identify and record the damage to the complex. The Cathedral is vast and expansive. We'll split up into four groups, each group composed of one archaeologist and one armed security member. Make sure you carry your hand-held radios and test them before you depart. Cell service in this area is not reliable. We'll meet back here at exactly three forty-five. Felix, you'll take the nave. Adolpho, you'll assess the eastern and southern basilicas. Ole, I want you to inspect the western and northern basilicas, and Sara, you'll survey the exterior. Are there any questions?" Wolfgang paused for a few seconds and then dismissed the group. "That's all."

Sara attempted to hide her disappointment in her assignment. From where she was standing, she could look into the nave and see the fallen pillar of St. Simeon. Finding something of interest on the outside grounds seemed farfetched. She returned to the SUV and grabbed a small red North Face backpack that held her camera, water, and snacks. The placid Saed was sitting in the driver's seat with his eyes closed.

"You and I are going to inspect the cathedral grounds," she said to Saed, who immediately went to the back of the SUV and retrieved an AK-47 and his own backpack.

"Do you really need that here?" she asked while pointing to the rifle.

"I hope not, but it's better to be safe than sorry."

The massive stone ruins of the church and monastery were copper in color. The wooden roof of the church and monastery buildings had rotted and collapsed centuries earlier. The walls, arches, and pillars that framed the structure were still largely intact. Surrounding the buildings were rolling hills covered with high grass, shrubs, and the occasional hibiscus tree. Large stones, each the size and shape of a small refrigerator, were scattered around the structures, seemingly at random. When it was constructed in 473 A.D., under the order of Emperor Zeno following the death of St. Simeon the hermit, it was the largest Cathedral in the world.

Sara began her inspection at the main entrance and began a slow survey counterclockwise around the cathedral. Waist-high grass sprinkled with red cardinal wildflowers made for a pretty view. The high grass also hid many of the fallen stones. Sara moved slowly and cautiously around the cathedral to avoid tripping and scraping her shins on the stones beneath the grass. She came across a bomb crater. She stopped and took photos of the car-sized hole in the ground, as well as some scarring on the exterior cathedral wall made by shrapnel from the blast.

It took an hour to reach the first basilica, which stretched like an arm two hundred yards from the main church building. Sara sat on a stone and retrieved a bottle of water from her backpack; Saed sat next to her and did the same. The cool morning was turning into a warm spring day. Sara could see a sheen of sweat on Saed's face. From the tip of the eastern basilica, she was able to see across the open field and observe the length of the northern basilica. In between were rolling green hills covered with the ubiquitous red wildflowers. The hill sloped gently away from the cathedral down to a valley where a smaller structure stood five hundred yards from the basilica.

"Those look like fresh dirt piles next to that building; let's go have a look," Sara said to Saed as she placed her pack back onto her shoulders. As the two walked down the hill and got closer to the building, they could see that it was a mausoleum with a small graveyard attached.

"Gravediggers," said Saed.

"Yes, I can see."

Sara athletically vaulted over the stone wall into the small cemetery. Saed took the long way around through the gate. The headstones were arrayed in lines; some were broken, many were very old, dating back to the fifth century, while others had dates on them that were much more recent. She walked over to the fresh earth and found two gravestones that were knocked over and partially covered with dirt. The writing on the stones was faded, but she could recognize enough to tell the language was Ottoman Turkish. Looking down into the nearest dug-up grave, she found bones and a clay pot. Curious about the pot, she decided to have a closer look. She was dropping her backpack to prepare for the climb down into the grave when she heard a call on the radio attached to her belt.

"Sara, are you there?" She heard Wolfgang's German-accented voice. She picked up the radio and pressed the transmit button on the side.

"This is Sara."

"I need you to come to the northern basilica; we've found something interesting and we need your help."

"I've found two graves that have been dug up in the cemetery," replied Sara.

"This is more important; please come immediately," Wolfgang stated.

Saed was just arriving at the gravesite as Sara was returning her backpack to her shoulders.

"We have to meet Doctor Boettinger in the north basilica."

Saed grimaced as he turned around and started to lumber back up the hill. Once at the top, Sara waited for her security man to catch up. She and Saed entered the basilica together where it intersected with the nave. They noticed a gathering at the far end of the basilica and went to it. Wolfgang met her, while Felix and Ole both remained huddled around a hole in the wall.

"What's going on?" asked Sara.

"Ole has made a most interesting discovery. Inside that niche there once was a series of statues depicting the ascension. The thieves used a crowbar and pried them from the niche interior. What's so interesting is that in doing so, they exposed a storage space behind the niche."

"What's inside?"

"Black lacquer boxes covered in writing. Very intricate gold calligraphy. We haven't opened them yet; we could use your Arabic skill."

Sara stood next to Wolfgang and watched Ole and Felix extract the boxes from within the hidden space. They handled the boxes gently, lined them up, and photographed them. Sara approached the first box on the end and studied it. The box was a perfect cube, two feet in every direction. The lacquer coating had a few cracks but otherwise showed little damage. Sara studied the writing.

"I thought my Arabic was passable, but I couldn't figure it out," Felix said as he walked up beside Sara and studied the box.

"It's Aramaic, East Syriac," Sara replied.

"That explains a few things. What does it say?"

"It says, 'The Holy Quran.'"

"The Holy Quran?"

"Yes, as in 'The' and not 'A' Holy Koran."

"Why would it be written in Aramaic?" asked Wolfgang, who was standing behind Sara and Felix.

"The language around Mecca at the time of Mohammed was Aramaic, and the first Quran was almost certainly written in the East Syrian dialect," answered Sara.

"This could be a significant find," said Wolfgang.

"Do you think we should open it and find out?" asked Felix, as he placed a second box down next to the first.

"We don't have the tools to open this box without damaging it. We should take it back with us and study it properly," Wolfgang said.

"What about this second box? What does it say it contains?" asked Felix.

Sara moved over to the second box and studied it for a full five minutes.

"This box contains 'The Stone'," answered Sara.

"Are you sure that's what it says?" asked Ole.

"Yes, I'm sure, although I have no idea what it means," replied Sara.

"This is intriguing. These boxes may contain important artifacts that have been hidden away for centuries. We'll take them back where they can be studied and safeguarded. Ole and Felix, please have them loaded into the vehicles. We head back immediately," said Wolfgang.

"Don't you think we should open them and confirm they are what you think they are before we abandon the task we came here to perform?" asked Ole.

Wolfgang paused for a minute. "Only if you think you can open them without causing damage," he said.

Adolpho had arrived moments earlier and listened to the conversation between Ole and Wolfgang. He removed a leather pouch containing a small set of archaeology tools from his jacket and approached the first box. Sara watched as he surveyed the box with one tool that looked like a pick and another that was a small mirror that resembled a dental tool.

"The box can't be opened without breaking the seal," Adolpho said.

"Break it," replied Felix.

"Yes, break it," said Ole.

"It's up to you," Adolpho said to Wolfgang.

"Go ahead. We would only do the same back at our camp."

Adolpho took a thin razor knife from his pouch and inserted it into the seam at the top of the box. He slid the blade through the wax-like substance sealing the box.

"What is that?" Felix asked.

"Bitumen, I think. It's been used as a seal since Roman times," said Adolpho

Adolpho ran the X-ACTO razor blade all the way around the lid of the box. He then signaled Sara to help him.

The two slowly lifted the top off the box. When the top separated from the rest of the box they heard the noise of a vacuum seal being broken.

"What's inside?" asked Ole, who was crowded out from view by the others.

Adolpho gently removed an object wrapped in black cloth from inside. He placed it on the box top in front of Sara. He began to unwrap the object. "It's a book, leather bound, probably deerskin or some such animal," he said.

"What does it say on the cover?" asked Ole.

"Same as on the box, 'The Holy Quran,'" Sara said.

"Could this be one of the originals made by Zayd ibn Thabit?" asked Felix.

"We would need to carbon date it to be sure. If it is, then it's thirteen hundred years old. We should put it back, regardless of who wrote it; it's very old, and the pages are too fragile to touch," said Adolpho.

"Whatever happened to the five original copies of the Koran made by Zayd ibn Thabit which were commissioned by the Caliph?" asked Adolpho.

"Five copies of the one true original were sent to the Muslim regions at the time; the location of three are known, and this may be one of the missing copies," answered Sara.

"Let's check the next box," Ole said.

Adolpho repeated the procedure. The group was expecting to find a stone under the cloth. Only this time, when the fabric was removed from around the object, what they found underneath was another box, this one the size of a toaster. Sara watched Adolpho strain and then signal for Felix to help him remove the surprisingly heavy box.

Adolpho once again went through the process of opening the box. Sara watched as he unwrapped the cloth from around a black, tablet-shaped stone

"What is it?" asked Ole.

"I have no idea, it's just a square, tablet-shaped stone," answered Adolpho.

"The Quran could be a significant historical find. Let's load up and get these archaeological finds to safety as soon as possible. Cataloguing the damage to the Cathedral is going to have to wait," said Wolfgang.

CHAPTER 3

Road to Homs

It was late afternoon by the time the trucks were loaded up and the convoy set off on the return trip to the Shirin compound on the outskirts of Homs. Sara was in the third SUV following behind Wolfgang, who was in the second vehicle. Ole was leading the convoy and Adolpho was trailing.

"Why are we stopping?" asked Sara

"Roadblock," replied Saed, as he removed a pistol from the storage console behind the gear shift.

"Are we in trouble?" asked Sara.

"The control of this road shifts all the time; it depends on whose roadblock it is," said Saed.

Up ahead, Sara could see two men pointing rifles at Ole's vehicle, while talking to Ole and his driver. The two men speaking to Ole had heavy beards and wore mismatched military vests and uniforms. Sara watched as the doors to the SUV were opened and Ole and his driver, whose name she did not know, got out. The two men signaled with their weapons for the personnel from the other vehicles to get out and come forward to the first vehicle in the convoy. Sara watched Saed open the car door and tuck his pistol under his shirt in his back waistband as he exited the truck.

When Sara and Saed approached the two soldiers, they were directed to stand with Ole, Wolfgang and the other two members of their team. They were close enough to the soldiers to hear them talk among themselves. The shorter one, who appeared to be the leader, was telling the tall one that, once they had everyone assembled, he would inspect the vehicles. The subordinate would guard the personnel.

The tall soldier kept his weapon oriented at the larger group, while the leader kept his weapon aimed at Adolpho and his driver who were still approaching. When Adolpho joined the group, the leader turned his attention to the first SUV and, for the moment, the soldier took his eyes off the group and watched the leader and not his charges.

The sound of a pistol discharging so close to her ear was a deafening surprise. It happened so fast, she didn't have time to react. Sara watched the soldier who was only five feet from her, the one who was supposed to be covering her group, drop like a sack of bricks after a bullet exploded the left side of his skull. Stunned, Sara turned her attention to the leader, who was opening the SUV door when the shot was fired. Before he could get both hands onto his weapon and raise it, five more pistol shots rang out in rapid secession. Sara watched the man fall dead to the ground.

"We need to get out of here, fast!" Saed shouted, with the smoking pistol in his right hand. Although she had trouble understanding the words because of the temporary ringing in her ears, the body language was obvious. All of the others began to run to their vehicles and she joined them.

Driving past the roadblock, Sara stared at the two bodies on the road as Saed swerved around them to keep up with the other vehicles in the convoy.

"Will you pass me a bottle of water?" asked Saed.

Sara's hands were shaking so badly that she had trouble opening the bottle for Saed. She finally handed the bottle to Saed and it disappeared in his big paw. She looked up at the big man and he looked as passive and docile as ever.

"Who were those men?" asked Sara.

"Al Nusra," replied Saed.

"What did they want with us?"

"Nothing directed at us— they were just collecting tolls, stopping vehicles, and collecting as much money as they can get. If they'd found the relics, they would've confiscated them. They also would've confiscated the trucks and taken us captive. I had no choice," Saed said.

Sara nodded.

"I just want to get back in one piece. Nothing was mentioned about gunfights when I signed up for this at the University."

Sara found herself focusing on Saed and his neatly trimmed beard and bald head the remainder of the trip back to the compound. He was as relaxed as she was tense. She could feel a familiar soreness in her jaw from a childhood habit of grinding her teeth when under stress.

The sun was setting when they passed through the guarded compound gate of the Shirin Headquarters. Sara silently said a prayer as the vehicle came to a halt.

The compound consisted of two villas in the outskirts of the Baba Amir neighborhood of Homs. The city was a major battlefield during the rebellion and had been secured by Assad's forces for more than two years, which was enough time to restore electricity and water to much of the area. Most of the buildings in the city had been reduced to rubble. Two years after the hostilities had ceased, the city was still mostly deserted, which allowed Shirin International to take its pick of properties offered by the Syrian Government. The villas were comfortably furnished.

Sara emerged from a hot shower, quickly dressed in a pair of jeans and a t-shirt and headed to the communal dining room with a voracious appetite. She grabbed a plate and headed through the buffet, which was stacked with Lebanese cold and hot mezza dishes. She joined Ole and Wolfgang at a table with her plate piled high with chicken kebabs, manakeesh (Lebanese pizza), falafel, tabbouleh salad, kofta meatballs, and baklava.

Ole did a double take when Sara dropped the heavy plate on the table.

"Did you forget you only weigh 50 kilos?" Ole asked.

"I can't remember when I've ever been this hungry or when food has ever tasted so good," Sara replied with a kebab in her hand.

"I think there was a point today when we all felt we had enjoyed our last meal," said Wolfgang. Nobody responded to that.

"Where's Adolpho?" asked Sara.

"He's in the lab with the artifacts," said Wolfgang.

"What's he up to?" said Sara.

"He brought a quadrupole mass spectrometer with him. He borrowed it from the University of Rome. He's conducting C-14 measurements," Wolfgang said.

"How long before we'll know how old the Quran is?" asked Sara.

"It will take two days according to Adolpho. His portable system is a huge improvement over the six weeks I'm used to with the ancient equipment at my University," Wolfgang replied.

"It's a very interesting find. Sara, since you're the only one with the language skills, you should check to see how the text deviates from the Uthmanic Codex. That should tell us a lot," Ole said.

"Like the Sanaa Quran, if there are any differences then we'll know it pre-dates the final approved version crafted by Zayd ibn Thabit at around 650 AD," Sara replied.

"Wouldn't it be marvelous if we discovered one of the early versions of the Quran?" Wolfgang asked.

"The Muslims believe there was only ever one version of the Holy Quran. Mohammed received the first revelation from the angel Gabriel in 610 AD. After each revelation, Mohammed would recite the message verbatim to his companions who would write it down, as Mohammed was illiterate. Because the Quran was revealed in disjointed verses and chapters, a point came when it needed to be gathered into a coherent whole text. There are disagreements among both Muslim and non-Muslim scholars as to when the Quran was compiled. Some believe Mohammad compiled it before he died, while others believe it was collected by either Ali ibn Abu Talib or Abu Bakr. Who knows, maybe the text we found today will help us understand this mystery?" Sara said.

CHAPTER 4

Homs Syria

Sara woke to the sound of gunfire. She was frozen in her bed, lying on her back in the dark, unable to decide what to do, too frightened to move. The door to her room flew open and she saw the silhouette of a man. It was a big man with a bald head.

"Come with me, we need to get out of here!" she heard from the familiar voice of Saed.

"I need my clothes." Sara was wearing only panties and a t-shirt.

"No time for that, come on!" Saed pulled at her arm. Sara managed to snag a pair of blue jeans and running shoes from the top of the bureau by the doorway as Saed pulled her into the hallway. Gunfire reverberated downstairs and from one of the bedrooms on the second floor. Saed led Sara down the hallway toward the back staircase when a man exited one of the bedrooms with a rifle. Saed shot the man before he could raise his rifle. Saed and Sara stepped over the man and ran toward the end of the hallway to the staircase.

They stopped, midway down the stairs, to listen, before trying to reach the door at the base of the stairs. Sara used the time to slip her jeans on and to step into her running shoes. They walked down the rest of the way and entered the kitchen. Two bodies were on the floor. Sara hesitated when she recognized them, and then followed Saed out the back door into the darkness of the courtyard. Without warning, Saed fired three shots with his pistol and she heard a weapon fire from inside the villa. She raced after Saed out into the courtyard that separated the two villas and around to the back of the Villa they had just left. When they reached the outer wall of the villa complex, Saed picked Sara up by the waist and lifted her over. Sara felt herself slide over the top of the stone boundary and managed to hang onto the edge before slowly dropping to the other side. Saed followed seconds later.

Out in the street, they ran toward a neighboring villa. The wall of the villa had been destroyed and most of the villa was bombed out. Saed led Sara through a hole in the wall into a dark empty building. The room was illuminated by the moon because most of the roof was missing. They found a staircase and walked down the stairs. Sara put her hand on Saed's shoulder and he guided her down into a basement. They reached the bottom and Saed led Sara to the edge of the room and the two sat down on the dirty tile floor.

Sounds of the massacre could still be heard coming from their villa. The spaces between the cracks of gunfire grew longer, and the ferocity of the violence had slowed. Minutes went by, and for longer and longer periods the only sound Sara could hear was her own breathing. She was too terrified to talk. Saed was quiet; he held the pistol in his hand and his attention was focused on the staircase they had used to get down into the basement. It was too dark to see the stairs, although they were only ten feet away.

Eventually, the gunfire stopped entirely. Sara was exhausted from the stress, sitting back to back with Saed, each leaning against the other, with him facing the stairs and Sara facing a wall. Neither spoke. Seconds ticked away, then minutes that seeped into hours.

"I don't hear anything. I think they've left," Saed whispered.

"What do we do now?" asked Sara

"We should go up and get help," Saed said.

"Can't you call someone from here?" asked Sara.

"I don't have my phone. When the attack started, I only had time to get my pistol and then I went for you."

"Are we going back to the Villa?" asked Sara.

"Only if it looks clear."

Saed stood in the darkness and held Sara by the arm helping her up. With the pistol in his left hand and using his right hand as a guide against the wall, he made his way toward the stairs.

As they approached the top of the stairs, they could see sunlight. Sara followed behind Saed with her hand pressed against his lower back as he stepped into the sunlight at the top of the stairs.

The crack of three shots echoed in the stairwell. Sara felt her companion's body jerk and then she felt the big man fall backward. Saed's falling knocked her off balance and the two tumbled backward down the stairs. Her head crashed against the basement floor and she lost consciousness.

She awoke in the back of an open truck and could feel a corrugated metal surface beneath her. She imagined it was a pickup truck. Her hands and feet were tied, and she had a gag in her mouth that tasted like motor oil. It was dark, hot, and difficult to breathe under the heavy tarpaulin draped over her; her head was pounding, and her mouth hurt from the tightness of the gag. She could hear traces of a conversation over the road noise. The language came as a surprise; it was Turkish.

After a what seemed like hours, the truck came to a halt. Sara was dragged out of the truck by her feet. Once her body cleared the truck bed, her back and head fell flat against a dirt surface and then someone grabbed her by the arms and, along with the person holding her feet, they lifted her and carried her into a building. She was taken into a room and then dropped hard onto the floor. Her feet and hands were untied. The two men left without speaking.

Sara removed the gag and then picked herself up off the ground. The room had an overhead light, but no windows. The only furniture was a bed. Adjacent to the bedroom was a small bathroom. She went inside and drank from the faucet and then washed her face with water. She tested the bedroom door, but it was locked. Sara sat on the edge of the bed and began to sob.

CHAPTER 5

Gozo Island, Malta

I propel myself with long, slow kicks through the cobalt-blue water, entering the oval-shaped cave opening with room to spare on either side of me. The filtered sunlight gradually fades to darkness until the only illumination that remains comes from the beam of my flashlight. The limestone walls close in around me as I advance until only a foot of space remains on either side. The dive computer on my wrist indicates a depth of 77 feet. The walls around me are a reddish brown, the water cool. I make a right turn and then have to angle my body to fit through a narrower opening. Beneath me is only two inches of water, and above, I can feel my air tank scrape the top of the cave when I kick. I move forward with my arms fully extended, holding a flashlight to guide my way and using my fins to propel me. I'm committed to the position because the tunnel is too narrow to return my arms to my side. I'm using short kicks because the narrow tube I'm swimming through is too confining for a proper leg kick.

The cave twists to the left, this time opening into a large, sphere-shaped chamber. I take advantage of the opportunity to stretch before continuing through a triangle-shaped entryway on the far side. The cave is not nearly as tight as before. The absence of light eliminates any possibility of plant life, although there is some black and orange discoloration on the rocks from whatever kind of micro-organisms exist in this environment. I check my pressure gauge and confirm that I still have enough air to continue. The cave drops sharply, and I angle my body into an L and swim straight down until it levels. A boulder is blocking my path. I survey the far side of the narrow opening with my flashlight and then I stow the flashlight. In complete darkness, I unclip and remove my buoyancy compensator and air tank and slip the vest-shaped rig through the small hole and follow behind it. I squeeze my body through; even though it's dark, I can sense I'm in an open area because I can feel a current. I don my BCD and tank by swinging them over my head and clip the straps together. I retrieve my flashlight from where it's been clipped to the BCD and turn it on. The chamber is huge; in the guidebook it was described as cathedral-sized and that wasn't an exaggeration. My flashlight beam isn't even powerful enough to illuminate the far wall or the bottom. I drift in an upright position in the cavern and turn to look back to where I entered. A flashlight blinds me, and then from behind the light, a neon-yellow wetsuit emerges from the underwater tunnel. The figure is small enough that the person is able to emerge from the tiny opening with equipment intact. The black vest and mask with yellow wetsuit remind me of a bumblebee. The lithe, hooded bumblebee diver swims to me, and in the underwater darkness, we show each other our air levels. It's time to turn back.

The route back is as cramped and claustrophobic as the route in. When I finally see the bright blue water on the other side of the cave exit, I quietly celebrate with a fist pump. With my air running low, I'm anxious to surface. Once the bumblebee catches up, I give the thumbs-up sign and we surface together. A school of sardines briefly surrounds us; it's a mini silver storm for a moment and then it's gone. Unlike the inside of the cave, we're surrounded by a kaleidoscope of color and sea life. Fish, eels, jellyfish, seagrass, and plants are everywhere. It's beautiful. After a brief safety stop, we break the surface and swim to my boat, the *Sam Houston*.

I toss my fins onto the hydraulic ramp and climb the ladder. Cheryl hands me her fins and air tank with BCD attached. We hose each other off with fresh water while still on the ramp. Cheryl turns her back to me and I help her unzip her wetsuit. She sheds her bumblebee suit and my heart stops. Cheryl turns and smiles. It's a dazzling flash of white, and she knows the effect she has on me. I stay back and clean and stow the equipment while Cheryl showers.

When I'm done with the equipment, I climb the stairs to the fly deck and move into my favorite perch with an ice-cold bottle of Heineken that I snag out of the small fridge on my way to the couch.

Cheryl appears in a bathrobe, sunglasses, and a floppy sun hat the size of a large pizza. She climbs onto the couch and gives me a hug.

"That was awesome; what did you think?" she asks.

"Traveling in tight spaces, moving blindly in the dark, never knowing when you're going to get stuck or lost, use up all of your air and drown. What's not to like about cave diving?"

"It wasn't that bad."

"Yeah, it kind of was."

"Next time, you choose the venue."

"I want to go to that place with the big underwater Jesus Statue."

"They put that in when the Pope visited. It's called, *Christ of the Sailors*, and it isn't far from here; it's midway between the two islands. If we go, there's a shipwreck nearby we can dive at the same time."

"We'll do that tomorrow; open water I enjoy. Caves, not so much."

On the table, my cell phone starts ringing. I look at the caller ID. It's Mike, so I pick up.

"I've been trying to get you for the past hour."

"Hi, Mike, how've you been?"

"No time for that. Where are you?"

"Gozo Island, Malta. I'm on the boat."

"I need your help with something."

"Ok, send it."

"We have an American college professor missing, possibly kidnapped in Syria."

"What's a professor doing in Syria?"

"Her name is Doctor Sara Salam, and she teaches Archaeology at the University of Pennsylvania. She was working with an NGO that was operating out of Homs with the approval of the Syrian Government."

"Homs is solidly under government control. Did Assad's people take her?"

"We don't know. There was an attack, and every member of her organization was killed. The bodies were found two days ago; hers was the only one not accounted for."

"How long ago was the attack?"

"Three days, tops. We don't have any assets in place. The information we have is coming from Shirin International, a Swiss-based NGO that's working to preserve Syrian Antiquities that are getting lost and destroyed because of the Civil War."

"Dying to save clay pots seems a bit silly, even for an Ivy League college professor. Why's the CIA involved? The only organization that should care about this one is the selection committee for next year's Darwin awards."

"She's not just a Professor; she's also Assistant Director of Middle Eastern Antiquities at the University of Pennsylvania Cultural Heritage Center. They have some clout. One of the board members of the Heritage Center is a big-time political donor and he's pressuring the White House."

"You've been working on this for two days. Have you found anything?"

"Not much. I'll send you what we have."

"Sounds good. I'll get the guys at Clearwater engaged. Can you provide ISR?"

"Satellite only; we don't have anyone on the ground, and all the UAV assets are committed."

"That'll give Dave something to work with."

"He never seems to need much. Some of our folks are starting to think Clearwater's capabilities rival our own."

"I think they may be better. I read an article yesterday in Fortune that said four hundred Google employees resigned because they wanted out of the same business Clearwater is in, which is combining artificial intelligence with intel sensor feeds. They even outed the black project, code name, 'Project Maven', being loyal San Francisco patriots and all."

"That's a Department of Defense project. Dave Forrest is way ahead of them, but he's not ahead of everyone."

"Send me what you have, and I'll start the search. I probably won't be able to go in-country for another day or two."

"Ok."

"Will we get any cooperation from the regime? Will they grant us entry?"

"No, they'll kill you if they find you."

"I was afraid of that."

"Do the best you can. I need to report some progress."

"Vacation's over," I said to Cheryl.

"I was eavesdropping. Forward me what you get from Mike."

"We'll head back to the main island and put you on an airplane to Paphos. It'll take me a day to get back with the boat. Hopefully, by then you'll have enough to give me something to work with."

CHAPTER 6

Paphos, Cyprus

I ran the *Sam Houston* at twenty-eight knots and covered the nine-hundred-plus nautical mile trip in a day and a half of nonstop sailing. It was late in the afternoon when I arrived at Paphos, Cyprus. Cheryl said they needed more time to analyze the situation, and because I hadn't slept, I was grateful for the delay. We scheduled an intel update the next morning. After I got done tying down and hooking up the yacht, I checked in with customs and walked over to the Moorings Restaurant for a late lunch. Paphos Harbor is very picturesque, with a medieval castle guarding entry to the harbor, and a big selection of quaint, locally owned restaurants and shops located along the waterfront.

The next morning, I was the last to arrive at the Clearwater conference room. Clearwater is a joint venture between GSS, a Scottish Company run by David Forrest, and Trident, my company. The Clearwater office is inside the Trident Hangar which can be found at Paphos International Airport. David Forrest runs Clearwater, and he's also a professor at the University of Edinburgh, a math genius, and a computer savant. Clearwater makes most of its money tracking down ships that fall off the grid for insurance companies and shippers. It also occasionally puts its unique artificial intelligence software to use for Trident's purposes.

I sat at the head of the table. Seated to my left was Migos, my wingman, in what we had begun to call Alpha Team. To my right was McDonald, my deputy. Next to Migos was Burnia, and seated beside McDonald was Jankowski. Burnia and Jankowski are on Bravo Team; Migos refers to them as the Bam Bam Brothers. Burnia and Jankowski are a pair of former CAG operators who are still very much in their prime. Migos is former Army Special Forces, and while I have the same background as Burnia and Jankowski, I'm definitely no longer in my prime. In the center of the table was a box of doughnuts; I helped myself to a powdered jelly. Cheryl handed me a cup of coffee and used a napkin to gently dab away my sugar mustache. The group was assembled.

Cheryl gave the briefing. It lasted for ninety minutes and provided details and photos of the Shirin International personnel who were killed in Homs. Shirin had been cooperative with the US government. They provided detailed information on the recent activities of the team, including their last trip to the St. Simeon Monastery. The briefing ended with the last known communications from Doctor Sara Salam.

"She called her Mother on the night of the attack. She said she was coming home because she didn't feel safe. Something happened on the trip back from St. Simeon that rattled her," Cheryl said.

"What about the local security they hired? What do we know about them?" I asked.

"The information we have on the Shirin personnel is from the governments of Germany, Switzerland, Italy, and Norway. No information has been provided on the Syrian citizens."

"We don't know how many of the locals were killed?" I asked.

"No, we don't," Cheryl replied.

"Do we know who they are? Has Shirin provided payroll information?"

"We have a list, but we don't know who was on duty."

"Is that everything? No imagery of the attack or movements to and from the Shirin Compound?"

"We don't have anything else."

"Migos and I will go in and check out the Shirin Compound and see what we can find. Any suggestions on how we get in?"

"I thought you were going to say that. The best option is to fly commercial from here to Beirut. Syria has normalized relations with South Africa, and we've already taken the liberty of obtaining the visas and documents for both of you. The border crossing to Beirut is open.

You can drive across with a flash of your South African passport. Homs is a two-hour drive from Beirut," Cheryl added.

"What about weapons?"

"We'll deliver them to you in-country," McDonald replied this time.

"How?"

"We'll fly them in on the VBAT and drop them to you."

"Really?"

"Yeah, Homs is less than a hundred and fifty miles from here. We'll put that boat of yours outside of Syrian waters and use it as a forward command center. If we need to get you, we can launch a RIB. We can range you with the VBAT UAV from the boat and if things get dicey we have the C-130s and the unmanned AH-6 and MH-6 that can reach you from this location in less than an hour."

"So far, the only part of this op that I like is that it's close to home," I said.

"What about us?" said Jankowski.

"You and Burnia will go with McDonald on the *Sam Houston*. Tow the RIB behind the yacht. If Migos and I need support, you can insert along the coastline and link up with us. Bring fuel in case we need to create a refuel point for the Little Birds."

"Will do."

"We have no idea how this is going to play out. Migos and I will poke around and find out what we can. When's the next flight to Beirut?"

"There's a forty-minute direct flight leaving from Larnaca in two hours."

"OK, get us to Larnaca and find a spot where you can drop us a couple of pistols by noon."

CHAPTER 7

Homs, Syria

I navigated with a portable GPS while Migos drove the rented Toyota Landcruiser. We stopped outside the gate of the Shirin International Compound. The streets were empty. Most of the villas and buildings in this part of the city are destroyed; the roads are littered with bricks, building debris, and burned-out vehicles. I stepped out of the SUV and felt a blast of desert heat. It was late in the afternoon and the sun was high and oppressive. It was eerily quiet; the only noise was from the occasional gust of wind as it whistled through the gaping holes in the surrounding structures. Migos opened the steel gate leading into the compound and I followed him inside.

"This place looks like a scene from one of those post-apocalypse movies," Migos said.

"It does have a Mad Max feel to it, doesn't it? Let's start with the building on the left."

The bodies were gone, but the signs of the slaughter were everywhere. Dried blood and expended shell casings littered the floor. We did a walk-through of every room.

"It looks like they caught them late at night or early morning. Most were shot in their bedrooms," Migos said. Only one of the bedrooms had girl clothes in it. I guessed it must have belonged to Sara. There were no electronics or jewelry; items of value must have already been looted. There was no shell casing on the floor of Sara's bedroom, which was a good sign. In the first villa, the clothing brands were all western, in the second, the clothes included some local.

"This must have been where the staff lived," Migos offered as we inspected the second villa.

"Probably. We need to find someone we can talk to. This is getting us nowhere."

"How?" Migos asked.

"I'm sure there are people living in this neighborhood. I don't imagine anyone can survive a civil war unless they know how to keep a low profile. Once the sun goes down, I'll bet we find some life."

"Let's move the vehicle inside the compound and wait," Migos suggested.

"Sounds like a plan."

We moved the vehicle through the gate and inside the walled area of the compound and spent the remaining daylight hours searching the first villa more thoroughly. The bullet casings were NATO caliber, which was different from what I'd expected. NATO casings meant they used M4s or M16s, which are rare in Syria as compared to the ubiquitous AKs that dominate the region. The first villa had a bedroom that was made into a makeshift lab. Surprisingly, the lab equipment had not been looted. It took a few phone calls back to Dave Forrest and Cheryl to figure out what the lab equipment was used for. The machine used for carbon dating was still turned on when we found it. The display was showing a reading of 1,386. There were no samples to be found anywhere of antiquities, or the find Sara had mentioned in the call she made to her mother.

Migos and I left the villa as soon as it got dark. We walked around the perimeter wall looking for neighbors. The smell of cooking fires wafted through the air, and we searched for the source. In one of the buildings, catty-corner to the Shirin Compound, we found two boys outside in the street. Migos approached them and started a conversation in Arabic. He offered the kids some of the candy we had purchased in the Beirut airport for exactly this purpose. Migos was quickly engrossed in conversation, while I hovered in the background. Eventually, the kids left.

"What did you learn?" I asked.

"A lot. The attackers didn't speak Arabic. They were speaking to each other in a language the children didn't understand. The kids said that after the firing stopped in the compound, there was more firing in that building over there. We should go have a look."

The building they pointed out was a partially destroyed villa. We used flashlights to enter the building; inside we found expended bullet casings on the first floor. On the stairs leading down to the basement, we found more dried blood. As we were exiting the villa, we saw several people moving around on the second floor of the villa next door. Unlike the Shirin Complex, not all of the other villas had power. The villa was dark as we approached the entry gate.

The gate was made of steel bars. Migos banged on the door and asked, in Arabic, if anyone was home. A man emerged out of the dark holding a rifle. Migos raised his hands and started talking in Arabic. After several minutes, the man opened the gate and ushered us forward, leading us inside the villa.

The windows were covered with fabric, and several candles provided minimal lighting. On the floor of the main room, I could see at least seven people sitting on cushions. Migos gave the man who brought us in a bag with the remaining dates, candies, and nuts we bought at the airport. The Mad Max existence lived by these people made them wary of strangers, especially westerners. Migos explained who we were and why we were in the area. I was able to follow some of the conversation, but my Arabic is too limited to lead it.

We left the villa two hours later and returned to the Shirin Compound.

"How are we going to find this guy?" asked Migos.

"He lives in the area. I say we just go around paying people for information until somebody points him out to us."

"We should go back into Lebanon and get more bargaining material."

"If we leave now, we'll get through the Al-Qaa/Jussiyeh border crossing before morning and we can come back tomorrow night."

We pulled out of the compound and headed back to Beirut in our SUV. I called Cheryl and put Clearwater to work searching for our man. Then I called Mike to give him an update.

"We have a lead," I said.

"What is it?"

"One of the Shirin International Security personnel was seen leaving the compound after the attack. We believe he was involved.

He's from a family that lives in the area, and we're working on finding him."

"What's his name?"

"Khaled Abadi."

"Anything new on the girl?"

"Most of the gunfire occurred in the bedrooms; it was a surprise attack while everyone was sleeping. No shots were fired in the lone female bedroom, which we assume was Sara's. We believe she escaped the compound during the attack and sought refuge in a neighboring villa."

"Did she get away?"

"We don't know yet. After the attack, neighbors reported gunfire in the nearby villa. We found signs of a gunfight and a lot of blood on the stairs leading down to the basement. The Syrian military had already removed the bodies of the victims, and if Sara was one of the KIAs, her remains should have been turned over with the rest of the Shirin personnel. It seems most likely she was captured since there was only one way out of that basement."

"So, what now?"

"Now we find Khaled Abadi."

"Do you think you can?"

"Migos and I are going to keep searching the neighborhood. Clearwater may have a better chance tracking him electronically. The people in Homs have no access to food, water, medicine or security, but they have cell service and the internet. Shirin's main office will have contact info on Khaled, including his cell, and if Migos and I don't find him, I'm betting David Forrest will track him down using his online signature."

"Good luck."

We slept all afternoon in a hotel in the north end of Beirut and made it across the Syrian border before last light. We had enough food to pass ourselves off as part of an aid agency and planned to work our way around the neighborhood until we found someone who knew where to locate Khaled Abadi. We were entering Homs when Cheryl called.

"We found him," she said.

"How?" I asked.

"WhatsApp. He sent a location-tagged picture of himself to a friend. I'm texting you the location now."

"How old is this location?"

"Less than thirty minutes," Cheryl replied. I started to plug the LONG-LAT into my GPS while we continued to talk.

"What do we know about his location?"

"It's a built-up area, mostly residential apartment buildings. Lots of bomb damage. There are several Syrian Army checkpoints within two city blocks."

"Do you have ISR?"

"Yes, we have a satellite feed, and the streets are clear except for the two checkpoints. We can see people on the roofs of some in the nearby buildings. The apartments are three to five stories high. We can pinpoint the building, but we have no idea what floor or what apartment you'll be able to find him in."

"Send us an image of what he looks like, so we can identify him."

"Already sent."

"OK, GPS says we'll be at his building in twenty-five minutes."

"What's the plan?" asked Migos.

"We'll just pull up to the apartment building and start knocking on doors," I said.

Cheryl helped us bypass a Syrian Army roadblock. Migos parked in front of the apartment building, which was on a corner and appeared to have only one exit.

"You should wait in the lobby while I start canvassing," Migos offered.

"Let's stick together. It looks like four apartments per floor and there are four floors," I replied.

Only one of the apartments on the first floor was occupied. The tenants were an older couple who appreciated the fresh fruit and dates we delivered. Neither recognized the image of Khaled Abadi I showed them on my phone.

Three of the second-floor apartments were occupied. No one in the first two apartments recognized Abadi. The family living in the third apartment recognized him. Migos knocked on the door and did all the talking, and gave his spiel in the doorway. He was talking to a man and his wife who looked to be in their thirties. Behind the man were two boys, about ages eight and ten. When Migos showed the picture, the father said he didn't know him, and the mother shook her head. The look of recognition in the eyes of the children was unmistakable. We gave them gifts and they closed the door.

"Let's go downstairs," I said, as we both ran downstairs to the lobby.

"I'll stay here while you go outside and make sure this is the only exit," I said to Migos.

The lobby was small, about twelve by twelve feet. An elevator and a stairway lead into it, and the stairway had a door that opened into the lobby. I stood against the wall between the elevator and the stairwell.

I called Migos on my cell. I put one of the earphones from my cell into my ear, and we kept the call open so I could hear him, and he could hear me. We assumed the couple would warn Abadi and he would make a run for it if he was still in the building.

"There's a small alley in the back with a fire exit. I'll wait here," he said.

The elevator never made a sound; it was probably broken. Eventually, I heard footsteps coming from the stairway. I watched the door swing open and saw a woman in a burka that covered her face, and a man, who was too old to be Khaled, leave. The male glared at me as he walked past, and I pictured the lady behind the black mask doing the same. I smiled and gripped the Walther PPQ 9mm pistol behind my back. Minutes later, I heard another set of footsteps, heavier and faster this time.

The door flung open and a man raced for the exit door. I caught him with three quick strides as he was opening the lobby exit on the far side of the room. I dragged him down onto the tile floor. I straddled him from behind, with my right arm wrapped around his neck and my left hand gripping my right forearm to lock in the chokehold. I still wasn't completely sure it was Khaled, because I'd yet to have a look at his face. When I felt the body go slack underneath me, I rolled the body over. I checked the image against the one on my phone Cheryl had sent earlier.

"I have him," I said to Migos.

"Moving to you," Migos replied.

By the time Migos arrived, I had tied Khaled's feet using his belt, and his hands using his shoelaces.

"Let's get him into the Landcruiser and get out of here," I said.

"Where to?" Migos asked.

"Let's go back to the Shirin Compound."

Migos drove with me and Khaled in the back seat. It took twenty minutes to reach the compound and even though Khaled had regained his faculties, he didn't say a word.

Migos pulled Khaled out of the vehicle and dropped him onto the sand in front of the vehicle where he was illuminated by the headlights of the still-running vehicle. I walked around the truck and looked down at the bound and kneeling Khaled. He was covered in sweat and his eyes were wide in fear.

"You speak English. You were a translator with Shirin, right?" I asked.

"What do you want with me?"

"We were sent here to find the girl. Where is she?"

"I don't know where she is."

"Let's back up a bit. Start with the trip to St. Simeon's Cathedral."

Khaled had a good memory. He told the full story about finding the two boxes, the return to Homs, and Saed's killing of the two men manning the roadblock. Khaled was a member of the Free Syrian Army. He told us he informed his Commander of the discovery of the ancient Quran and the stone. He was on guard duty the night of the attack; he was the person who let the attackers into the compound.

"What about the girl? What happened to her during the attack?" I asked.

"Saed rescued her and took her out of the compound. The men went searching for her and found them in the villa over there," he pointed.

"What happened then?" I asked.

"Saed was killed. Dr. Salam was taken."

"Where was she taken?" I asked.

"I don't know."

"Who took her?" I asked.

"The Turks, Grey Wolves, not Free Syrian Army."

"How do you know it was Grey Wolves?" I asked

"They were Turkish. The only Turks in Syria are Grey Wolves and the Turkish Army. The Turkish Army wears uniforms, but these men didn't."

"Where do we find these Grey Wolves?"

"North, all Turks are in the north. They never come this far south. I had no idea any of this was going to happen. I worked for Shirin as an interpreter and as security. I made periodic reports to the FSA. I was ordered by the FSA to allow access, and I did. I was told nothing about a slaughter and nothing about the Grey Wolves. Most of the people around here are FSA. I thought my people were going to take back the artifacts, nothing more."

"Why would the FSA be working with the Grey Wolves?" I asked.

"We never work together. Although we're both part of the Brotherhood, we're not allies, but we're not enemies either. The Grey Wolves concern themselves only with Turkey. I don't know why they did this thing."

"We're going to need to talk to your Commander. We need to know his Grey Wolf contact."

"I can't give that to you. If my Commander knew I'd spoken to you, he would have me killed. I have a family."

"If you give us the information we need, we'll give you some money and you can make a run for it with your family. If you don't, then I'll get the information out of you the hard way, and then I'll kill you. The choice is yours," I said.

Khaled looked at me; he had a survivor's mentality. A possible death in the future beats an immediate, certain death every time, and from my tone, he had to know he was facing a certain death if he didn't do as he was told.

We confirmed the information he gave us on his Commander with his cell phone data. I gave Khaled ten thousand Euros and dropped him off outside his apartment. I expected in a month or two he'd be living large in Germany or Sweden on the taxpayer's dime. I kept his cell phone.

Cheryl guided us around another roadblock and helped us find Khaled's Commander's villa. It was as he described it. The Commander was a man of significantly more means than Khaled. The villa was a home more fitting for a prosperous merchant than for a military man. We drove up to the tall metal gate and knocked.

A guard opened a peephole in the gate.

"Who are you and what do you want?"

"I'm here to see Mouloud Zetar," Migos responded in Arabic.

"What about?"

"He's expecting me. Tell him Khaled Abadi is here to see him."

Minutes later the door opened. The text Khaled had sent earlier requesting a meeting had done the trick. I drew my pistol, and as soon the door was open enough to expose the guard, I shot him. Migos took out the second guard who was positioned behind the first. Migos and I each took a rifle from the dead guards and ran toward the front door of the villa.

The heavy wooden door looked formidable. Migos got there first and tested the doorknob; it was locked. I slung the rifle over my shoulder and scaled the villa wall. The building was made out of heavy stones, with solid handholds. I climbed over the balcony rail and pulled Migos up behind me. I kicked in the balcony door and we entered an empty bedroom. I walked through the bedroom and entered into a dimly lit hallway. Gunfire erupted in front of me. I dropped to the prone on the hallway floor and returned fire. Migos jumped over me and entered the bedroom on the other side of the hallway. I heard a woman screaming from inside the bedroom Migos entered. Another extended burst of automatic gunfire came from the far side of the hallway. I could see thin arms sticking a weapon into the hallway and firing blindly in my direction. An entire magazine of bullets went over my head. When the gun was withdrawn, I assumed to reload, I jumped up and rushed forward. When I reached the corner of the hallway the gunner was behind, I swung my weapon and smashed the buttstock of my AK into the head of the shooter who was still fumbling with a magazine to reload.

Migos came up behind me and looked down at the gunman. It was a boy, no older than fourteen.

"That must be his son," Migos said.

"Must be," I replied.

The next two bedrooms we checked were empty. When we reached the last room in the hallway, bullets fired from inside the room splintered the wooden door. I waited for the shooting to stop.

"Mr. Khoury, we have your son and your family; they're alive. There is no need for anyone to die. We came for some information about an American woman. Don't make us turn this into a blood-bath," I said.

"I don't know anything about an American woman," a muffled voice said in English from behind the door.

"You have the answers we need. I'm going to give you a choice. Either sit down and talk with us or I'll burn this villa down with everyone in it."

A full minute passed. "I'm coming out. Don't shoot."

Mohammed Khoury was a heavy man. He had a thick, black beard and fat, partially bald head. When he saw his son lying on the hallway floor, bleeding, he rushed over to him. He picked his head up and, realizing he wasn't dead, cradled his head on his lap.

"What have you done? He's a twelve-year-old boy."

"You set up a massacre of Shirin International and the kidnapping of an American, Doctor Sara Salam. I want to know who took her and where."

"I don't know where they took her. I have no idea where she is."

"Who took her? I want a name," I said, menacingly pointing my rifle at him.

"I don't know the name of the people who took her."

"Let's start with the person you gave the information to."

"Omer Aslan."

"What information did you give him?"

"I told him Shirin had made a discovery. An ancient copy of the Holy Quran. He's a collector, a wealthy man. I wasn't expecting violence; I had no idea. My plan was to take the book and sell it to him. He thought it better to take it himself."

"Khaled Abadi said you were his Commander."

"I am, but I pay him for information to keep tabs on the people he guards. I have many others like him—that's my business. The SFA is a political movement, no longer active in fighting, as the war is over."

"How do we locate this Omer Aslan? Tell me everything you know about him."

CHAPTER 8

Paphos, Cyprus

The group was seated around the conference table. For some reason, everyone seemed to always sit in the same place.

"We just need a few more minutes," Cheryl said to the assembled group.

"How was Syria?" Roger asked.

"It was pretty dicey. Pat went all Tier-1 operator on a twelve-year-old kid; you should've seen it, the full Rambo," Migos said. I tried my best to make myself invisible while everyone at the table turned to glare at the child abuser.

"He was big for his age. He easily could've passed himself off as an eighth grader," I lamely replied. My joke fell flat, and even Cheryl was eying me with suspicion. "I didn't shoot him. I butt stroked the boy, and he was shooting at me with an AK, on full auto; he could've killed us both. I'm lucky to be alive."

Just then David Forrest came into the conference room. Salvation at last.

"We've found Dr. Salam; she's in Northern Syria, in a village named Salwah. The village is twenty miles northwest of Aleppo and only three miles east of the Turkish border." The display screen showed a map of Northern Syria, with Salwah in the center.

"We've pinpointed her to this farmhouse. We have imagery and phone intercepts confirming her presence." The imagery on the display screen showed an overhead of the farm.

"She's being held in this outer building. Each morning at around six she's moved to the main building. Every evening at around ten she's moved back. As you can see, she has a guard escorting her each time, but she's not bound."

"How did you find her?" I asked.

"Omer Aslan was the key. Once you gave us his name and contact information we were able to request COMINT and SIGINT support from the CIA. He's a bigwig and he's already on the watch list; U.S. Intel was already collecting on him. We were able to location track his communications into Syria, which narrowed the search considerably. Eventually, we confirmed her location with outbound signal intercepts from where she's being kept and imagery."

"What's the security situation in the area?" I asked.

A Turkish Mechanized Infantry Brigade is operating in the area. They're split up along twelve combat outposts arrayed in a semicircle around Idlib. It's a half circle, with the base being the Turkish border. The nearest combat outpost is in Salah. It's a company-sized force, composed of ten Leopard II tanks and eight ACV-15s with infantry, and approximately one hundred personnel. The next closest one is north of the St. Simeon Cathedral—it's another company-sized armor force. Around the farm, they have roving patrols and a guard post. Usually, there's a team of two walking the perimeter and two guarding the entry to the property. We have no way of telling how many security personnel are inside the farmhouse and the outbuildings.

"What's your best guess on the force guarding the farm?" I asked.

"Eight to ten personnel."

"Do they have air defense capability?" I asked.

"The Turkish military will have a robust air defense missile capability. The Grey Wolves themselves won't have anything but small arms."

"Who are they? Any idea on their training and background?"

"Grey Wolves?" replied David Forrest.

"Yeah, what's a Grey Wolf?" asked McDonald. Cheryl responded:

"Bozkurt or Grey Wolves are Turkish ultra-right nationalists. They've been around a very long time— since the sixties. Back then, they were supported by the CIA because they were staunchly anti-communist, which, at the time, was the only pre-requisite for CIA support. They've since been divorced by the Agency.

"They were behind the assassination attempt on Pope John Paul II in 1981, and the Taksim Square Massacre in 1977. They're considered a terrorist threat in all of the European countries with a large Turkish population, especially Germany.

"The organization's ideology emphasizes the early history of the Turkish states in Central Asia and blends it with Islam. One of their mottoes is, 'Your doctor will be a Turk and your medicine will be Islam.' Their ideology is based on the superiority of the Turkish race and nation, which they define as Sunni-Islamic and only inhabited by the Turks. They seek to revive the Turkish empire.

"Turkey's President Erdogan recently drew a lot of attention when he gave the Grey Wolf sign at a rally. Populism is growing in Turkey. They work closely with Turkish intelligence, and they're very active in Europe and Asia, especially in China. They're racist thugs."

"I'm less interested in the ideology and more in the tactical. Can they fight?" I asked.

"Yes, they can fight. The men guarding Sara will have combat experience. They'll most likely have served in the Turkish military and fought with the Grey Wolves in places like China, the 'Stans, and in Syria. Their sworn enemies in Syria are the Kurds and the Iranians."

"We'll go in tonight," I said.

The C-130 lifted off at 8:00 p.m. Four of us—Migos, Jankowski, Burnia and I—were wearing HALO rigs. We were all carrying DD M4s, the 300 blackout models with the integrated suppressors. Our Trident planes overfly Syria several times each week on delivery runs to Iraq. I decided to take advantage of our routine air route and use it to make a parachute drop.

I watched Burnia spread eagle into the night sky followed by Jankowski, Migos, and then myself. Even though it was May, the temperature at twenty-five thousand feet was well below freezing. I lost Burnia in the clouds. I descended into a cloud and pulled the ripcord at five thousand unable to see anything except my illuminated altimeter. I looked down at the GPS attached to the NAVAID on my chest and steered into the direction of the arrow until I was on course. Seconds later, I broke out of the cloud and spotted Burnia five hundred yards below and ahead of me. I stopped paying attention to the GPS and focused on chasing him. I watched him turn ninety degrees into the wind and I waited until I got to roughly the same spot in the air and did the same. I pulled both toggles down hard and flared my chute, landing only ten yards behind Migos.

I unclipped from my harness and strapped the small pack I had carried below my NAVAID over my body armor vest onto my back. I detached my rifle from the side of my harness and dropped my AN-PVS 31s night vision goggles on my helmet into position in front of my eyes. We were in a walnut farm, surrounded by rolling hills and trees. Our drop zone was a narrow dirt trail that went through the center of the orchard.

I took the lead, with the other three behind me in a column. The road crested a hill that overlooked the farmhouse and the two smaller buildings. The four of us stopped at the crest of the hill. From our vantage point, I could see two men walking along the short stone wall that bordered the farmhouse and the outbuildings. We were over one hundred yards away from the wall, and through my night vision, I could see both guards had rifles slung over their shoulders. One of the men was smoking. I knew from the satellite reconnaissance that there would be another patrol on the other side of the farmhouse guarding the driveway entrance to the house.

Migos pulled a pair of thermal binoculars out of his backpack. We moved down the hill toward the farm another ten yards and settled behind some shrubbery and waited. I was sitting, facing downhill with my back against my pack and my rifle on my lap. I had a clear view of the farmhouse and the smaller building we had seen the guards take Sara to on the satellite feed. Next to the other building that looked like a garage were parked two vehicles—a van and a pickup truck. Jankowski was carrying the hotwire kit; one of those vehicles was going to be our way out.

It was a warm and humid spring evening. The cloud cover acted like a blanket for the heat. I was sweaty from the weather and because of the warm gear I still had on from the jump. I ditched the over-pants and coat, but I still had on thermal underwear. A security patrol passed in front of us four times; there were two different teams walking the same perimeter route. The farmhouse blocked the view of the gate that was guarded by another team that stayed in place while the other team roved. Lights were on in all three of the buildings.

The farmhouse back door opened. A girl emerged with a guard walking behind her holding a rifle. "Burnia, you take the guard with the PC; Jankowski and Migos, take the rovers," I whispered into my throat microphone. IR laser marks instantly appeared on all three targets. Before I could stand, I heard three metallic-sounding discharges of suppressed fire to my left. Suppressed supersonic fire is only about thirty decibels quieter than normal fire, but it makes a huge difference. All three targets were down and being re-engaged by my team to make sure they would stay down. The girl remained standing, confused and unsure of how to react in the center of the open yard. I ran down the hill.

"Stay where you are! We're Americans here to get you out!" I said in a voice loud enough for her to hear me from fifty yards away. I hoped she was the only one who heard me. I could hear the other three guys bounding down the hill behind me.

"Are you Doctor Sara Salam?" I asked when I reached her.

"Yes," she replied.

"Get in the truck, we're here to take you home," I said while pulling open the passenger side door. Jankowski opened the driver's side door and was getting ready to hotwire the Toyota Hilux.

"Keys are in the ignition," I said.

I put Sara in the middle and hopped into the passenger side of the pickup truck. Burnia and Migos jumped into the cargo bed in back.

"Shoot the van tires," I instructed over my radio. The truck started and the two exposed tires on the van parked next to us exploded. Seconds later, as we were backing up, the door to the house opened. Migos and Burnia immediately opened fire on the farmhouse. Jankowski threw the pickup into drive and hit the gas. Jankowski kept his night vision on and the headlights off as we rounded the farmhouse and raced for the stone gate. I had my M4 out the window pointing it ahead of our path. The laser was bouncing around on the road in front of us while I looked through the windshield with my night vision goggles for the gate guards.

As soon as we turned the corner, the guards came into view, and I opened up with a ten-round burst on automatic. Both guards dove for cover behind a wall and disappeared from my view. I could hear Migos and Burnia putting out a high volume of fire. The truck flew past the gate. I stuck my head out the window, looked back, and saw both guards were lying on the ground either hit or too terrified to move. Red tracers from machine gun fire split the sky in front of us as we turned onto the road from the driveway. The men inside the house were too late; Burnia and Jankowski kept the machine gunner's head down with a steady rate of return fire until we were out of range.

I navigated with the GPS while Jankowski handled the wheel. We drove west to the village of Kah on a narrow dirt road with high embankments on both sides. We raced along the road in the dark with our headlights still off. Jankowski turned hard left and headed due south. We were paralleling the Turkish border less than a mile to our west. After another two miles, we turned right onto a dirt trail. Jankowski had to slow down to navigate the difficult path. Sara sat silently between Jankowski and me with her hands folded across her chest.

"My name is Pat, this is Stan. Are you up for a walk in the hills?" I asked Sara.

"Yes, I can walk." I handed her a bottle of water and a power bar. "You're going to need some energy; once we stop, it's three miles over some fairly rough terrain." I looked at her feet and saw that she was wearing running shoes, which I took as a good omen. She took the water.

"I'll be OK."

The trail turned from dirt to stone and eventually became too rocky to continue. Jankowski stopped the truck and we all got out and continued on foot. We entered a ravine and when we neared the end of it, Burnia stopped the patrol. I was in the back of the column of five and I went forward to have a look.

"Border guard," I heard Burnia say over my headset.

"Is he moving?" I asked.

"No."

"Do you have a shot?"

"Yes."

"Let's go back and circle around the next hill to the south where the guard can't see us breach," I said.

"Easier to just take him out and cut through the fence here," Jankowski said.

"It is, but he's not one of the bad guys, and if his body gets discovered before we're out of Turkey it could complicate our exfil."

I took the lead and brought everyone back a hundred yards and around the steep slope of a rocky hill. Sara kept falling, but she never complained. Finally, we reached the fence line. I stopped to survey for border guards. The area was clear.

Burnia went forward with a set of bolt cutters. Migos and Jankowski covered him.

"Breach complete," came over the comms, and we all began moving again toward the hole in the chain link fence.

After we crossed the border, we hiked for another mile and a half across open farmland. We stayed in the low ground and eventually reached the outskirts of a small Turkish village.

"McDonald, where are you?" I said over the radio. A set of head-lights came on across the field.

"Gotcha."

We all climbed into the van and McDonald pulled away. It was 3:00 a.m. by the time we reached the small port of Cevlik Plaji. The *Sam Houston* was tied up across from a lighthouse. We concealed our weapons and gear in nylon bags and deposited them onto the boat.

I took Sara downstairs.

"Sara this is your stateroom. I suggest a shower. Fresh clothes are on the bed. Plenty of food upstairs in the galley; we'll sail in a few hours."

"Why don't we leave now?" she asked.

"The Turkish Government isn't cooperating with us on this and leaving port this early in the morning will be conspicuous. Best to leave when all of the fishing boats head out for the day."

"Can I make a phone call?"

"I'm sure your family is worried sick about you, but it's safer to wait until we're outside of Turkish waters."

"OK."

"You should get some rest. When we get to our next location, some people are going to want to ask you a lot of questions."

At dawn, I was sitting on the fly deck. Across the water from our location, next to the lighthouse, was a huge stone building with a sign saying, "Turkish Coast Guard." McDonald returned the rented van. I noticed the first few commercial fishermen were making their way out of the harbor. I engaged the engines and fell in behind them.

I called Mike using the encrypted cellphone app on my phone.

"We have the PC, departing Cevlik Plaji as we speak," I said.

"Is the girl all right?"

"She's in good shape. McDonald had a quick look at her. She has a big bruise on the back of her head from a fall when she was captured, but otherwise no physical issues."

"Did she tell you anything about her capture?"

"I didn't ask. I thought you'd have someone at Paphos to debrief her."

"I do."

"We'll be there in five hours. I'll make sure she's rested and fed by the time we turn her over to you."

Two hours later, McDonald took the helm so I could go down and eat breakfast. We were in international waters and everyone was relaxed. I entered the salon and saw Migos and Sara working at the stove. Burnia and Jankowski were across from them on a bench seat at the galley table. I poured myself a cup of coffee.

"Sara, if you want to make some calls, it's OK," I said, holding up the phone. She dropped the spatula and took the phone.

"Thank you."

"It only works outside; it's a satellite phone." She walked toward the salon door onto the stern deck.

"Migos, go with her. Show her how to use it. Remind her not to say anything operational." I took over the stove and finished the omelets. We were eating when Sara returned the phone to me. Her eyes were moist, but she looked relaxed and content.

"Did you call your parents?" I asked.

"Yes."

"Are they OK?"

"Still very upset. They want to know when I'll be home."

"We'll be in Paphos in three hours. The intel people want to talk to you and then you'll be free to fly home."

"Why do the intel people want to talk with me?"

"I don't know. They probably just want to know why you were taken."

"I was taken because they needed someone to translate the Quran."

"Did you?"

"Most of it; I was two-thirds done."

"Why couldn't they do it themselves?"

"They were Turks. The Quran I was working on was written in Aramaic—Syrian Aramaic."

"What's so special about that Quran?"

"It's old, and it's a little different from the Quran of today."

"In what way?"

"In the references to the Qibla, which is the direction in which Muslims pray. In the Uthman Quran, which is the only one used by all Muslims, there are several references to the Qibla. One passage of the modern Quran discusses how there used to be multiple Qiblas but now there is only one. Another reference refers to Jerusalem and how it's no longer the direction to pray. A final passage refers to Mecca as the Qibla. The Quran we found at St. Simeon has only one reference to the Qibla, and it states that Al-Masjid Al-Aqsa is the rightful Qibla."

"Where is that?"

"Jerusalem."

"That's it? Your companions were killed, and you were kidnapped so the Grey Wolves could get their hands on a translated Quran that called Muslims to pray facing Jerusalem?"

"I don't think that's why they attacked us. Because when they stole the Quran and kidnapped me they didn't know what was in it. All they could have known was that it was very old and very valuable."

"How old was the Quran you were translating?"

"I don't know. We were having it carbon dated when the attack occurred."

"We saw the number 1,386 on the mass spectrometer when we searched your villa. Is that the date of the book?"

"No, that's how many years ago it was created from when the C-14 reading was taken. The date of the book would be the current year, minus 1,386." She did the math in her head. "632 AD, which would be about right if it was one of the early Quranic texts."

"What was the Grey Wolf plan for the book? Were they going to sell it? Is there a market for old Qurans?"

"It would be very valuable— priceless even. But I don't see any political value to the Grey Wolves."

"They also took the stone."

"What's that?"

"A black, square stone that we found in the same hidden space as the Quran."

"The Kaaba?" I asked.

"The Kaaba stone is broken up into seven pieces and is held together by silver. This stone is intact. There's only one Kaaba, and that's in Mecca."

"Did your captors ever communicate a reason for why they wanted an old Quran and a rock?"

"No, they hardly ever spoke to me. I was told to translate, or they would hurt me, so I translated."

"You're safe now," said Migos, putting his hand on Sara's arm.

Burnia turned to Jankowski and said, "Can you believe this? Migos is hitting on our precious cargo."

"I'm not hitting on our PC; I'm just offering comfort. I'm show-ing empathy," replied Migos.

"That's creepy Migos. Seriously, nobody does that," Jankowski said.

"Migos is being a gentleman. You shouldn't make fun of him," Sara said.

"We've rescued more than a few people. You're the first Migos has empathized with. Definitely the first he's helped out on the stove. He normally avoids work in any form," Burnia said.

"Don't forget the touchy-feely arm stroking; he's definitely hitting on a kidnap victim. Has he told you yet about how he got his nickname, Muey Muey Migos?" asked Jankowski.

"Ignore them Sara; they in live my shadow. Sometimes they get so jealous they act inappropriately. You should see them in social situations. When either of these two tough guys has to talk to a girl, they stammer and they stutter. It's painful to watch. Picture Urkel at a sorority party. I can't even be polite to a woman, and they think I'm hitting on her. It's very sad."

I saw Sara smiling, something I bet she thought she would never do again. I went back upstairs to spot McDonald on the helm.

CHAPTER 9

Abu Dhabi, UAE

I waited at Bentley's at the Galleria Mall in Maryah Island, Abu Dhabi, for Mike to arrive. I was seated by the bar, next to a window overlooking the water. Bentley's has a bar whose ambience would do justice to aficionados of alcohol-serving sanctuaries in any major city. I nursed a beer while gazing out the window toward a thin strip of beach only two hundred yards away. The beach belonged to the Beach Rotana Hotel. Up until a couple of years ago, the Beach Rotana had a great view of the Arabian Gulf. Property rights aren't a big thing in Arab monarchies. Maryah Island was constructed directly across from the hotel. The mall, hotel, and office buildings on the island now tower over the narrow strip of sand abutting the hotel. From my vantage point, the sunbathers resembled specimens at a zoo. It made me feel a little uncomfortable, so I couldn't imagine how they felt. Fortunately, it would be dark soon.

A young Pinoy hostess approached the table with Mike in tow. I stood to greet him.

"What's good here?"

"Start with the mac and cheese truffle or dynamite shrimp, and then go with the American Ribeye."

"Mac and cheese, like Kraft Dinner?"

"Nothing like that. And the steak is the best in Abu Dhabi; you can cut it with your fork."

"OK."

"Did you come through the hotel or the mall entrance?"

"Mall."

"What do you think of the place?"

"Definitely not a shopping destination for humble civil servants."

50

"It's crazy. It must be the highest concentration of the most expensive stores in the world."

"It looks like the only people who shop at this mall are locals."

"They're pretty much the only ones who can afford it. When you look at the mall shoppers, it reminds me of dominoes."

"Why dominoes?"

"The only two colors are black and white; the men are all in white kanduras and the woman are in all black abayas. Think of the irony. Every outrageously expensive designer clothing label in the world is located in this tiny little chichi mall, and the only people who shop here are monochromatic. Not only limited to black and white, but they can only wear two styles of clothing, one for boys and one for girls."

"Who's buying all the flashy designs with the fancy labels?"

"They are, but they can't wear them except when they travel."

"It's hard to understand these people sometimes. A mystery wrapped inside a riddle or something like that."

"Churchill's line about the Russians. It is a riddle, wrapped in a mystery, inside an enigma. Speaking of which—did you ever figure out why a Turkish hate group stole an old holy book?"

"We have a theory."

Mike waited for the wine steward to serve the wine before continuing.

"The Quran and the stone have been delivered to Hamas."

"How do you know that?"

"Reliable human source."

"Why?"

"To attack Saudi Arabia."

"I don't follow; explain?"

"The average American believes the big conflict in the Middle East is between the Arabs and the Jews.

"People familiar with the Region understand a conflict of almost equal magnitude exists between the Sunni and Shia Muslim Sects.

"There is a third Muslim conflict that gets much less attention in the West, and that's the fight between the two major Sunni groups, the Wahhabis and the Muslim Brotherhood," Mike said.

"It gets hard to keep all of the acrimony straight. They say Irish Alzheimer's is when you forget everything but the grudges. But, compared to the Arabs, the Irish are the most forgiving people in the world."

"Exactly, which is why the Saudis and Emiratis are on a slow simmer towards war with Turkey and Qatar at the moment."

"Who's going to win?" Pat asked.

"The Muslim Brotherhood has a more popular message for the masses. On the other hand, the Wahhabi message is better funded with petro-dollars. The Brotherhood is growing, and they've won elections in Turkey, Palestine, and Egypt. It's a more persuasive message-classic class warfare and wealth redistribution. Of the two Salafist groups, the Brotherhood is much more practical politically than Wahhabism; that's why the Arab Spring and the democratic elections that followed swept the Brotherhood leaders into office."

"What's the story on the Quran and the rock?"

"The conflict between the Saudis, the UAE, and the Brotherhood has been steadily building. They've cut off most trade to Turkey. Erdogan, the Turkish President, has been getting into some hot arguments with the both the UAE and Saudis. In the past, the Saudi-UAE coalition used military and financial support to reign in the Brotherhood movement in Egypt and Palestine. Since that hasn't worked, they're escalating. They have a complete embargo of Qatar. The latest plan is to build a moat around Qatar; can you believe that?"

"I heard. That's unreal—a forty-mile canal cutting them off from the Arabian Peninsula."

"The conflict is not only external. MBS, the new Saudi Crown Prince, is making a lot of enemies with his liberalization of the culture— movie theaters, relaxed dress codes, reigning in the religious police. Many of the Muslim faithful are now openly questioning if the Saudi leadership is worthy of the honor of being the keeper of the faith and protector of the twin Holy Cities of Mecca and Medina."

"I know many people in the region think Ibn Saud was a British lapdog. They believe King Abdullah, who's a direct descendant of the Prophet Mohammed, should be the one to reign over what is now called Saudi Arabia."

"Exactly. They believe the Hashemites are the rightful owners of Arabia, and that the British betrayed them and supported Ibn Saud when he forced them into Jordan. They think the Saudis are weak puppets of the West and are growing weaker. They see the recent liberalization as evidence of this weakness. The improved relations between Saudi and Israel are considered even further proof of this. Many Muslims are furious that the Saudis were silent when the US moved our embassy to Jerusalem."

"So how do an old book and a rock fit in?"

"We think there is a move afoot, led by the Brotherhood, to move the Qibla to Al-Masjid Al-Aqsa in Jerusalem. They'll use the Quran discovered in St. Simeon Cathedral as the religious justification. They'll also emplace the stone discovered at the Cathedral at the Al-Masjid Mosque. They'll claim it's the sister stone to the one in Mecca."

"Is it?" Pat asked.

"The Kaaba stone has never been analyzed. Supposedly, it came from a meteorite. But nobody knows. Muslims believe the stone was originally white and became black because it absorbs the sins of those who touch it. The claim that it's the sister stone can't be proved. However, the provenance of the artifacts from St. Simeon is pretty solid; they definitely originated in Mecca. Most likely, the items were moved from Mecca by the Ottomans. Why and when is still a mystery, but it doesn't matter. If the imams loyal to the Brotherhood across the Muslim world declare Jerusalem as the new Qibla, it's very possible much of Islam will follow."

"Why?"

"The only reason 1.3 billion pray facing Mecca every day is because they believe Allah told Mohammed to in a revelation. If a book that predates the Uthman Quran has a revelation from the Almighty that says otherwise, that might change things. The reason the Qibla was moved to Jerusalem temporarily during Prophet Mohammed's time was because a hostile invading force was occupying Mecca. Some already argue that the corrupt Saudi regime is a hostile force to the faith, so if shifting to Jerusalem is what was done during a hostile occupation before, why not now?"

"Why do we care if half of the Muslims face Jerusalem and the other half face Mecca?"

"If that's all that happened, we wouldn't. We think that might be enough to touch off another Arab-Israeli war."

"Who is 'we'?" I asked.

"The State Department, the C.I.A, even some of the allies we've consulted."

"What's being done?"

"Diplomacy, mostly. We know there's an information campaign being waged among the religious leaders and there are efforts being made to counter it."

"Where are the book and the stone now? You said Hamas had them."

"Hamas is another Brotherhood affiliate, and both are in Jerusalem somewhere."

"What's going to happen next?"

"A bunch of Sunni clerics is going to announce Al-Masjid Al-Aqsa as the new Qibla, and then all hell is going to break loose."

"Do the Saudis know all of this is going on?"

"Yes, we told them."

"Maybe the Saudis should make nice with the Brotherhood. Bury the hatchet, so to speak."

"They're having difficulty keeping their own people under control. A good chunk of their own population doesn't believe the Saudi leadership is worthy. Possible scenarios of how this plays out include a civil war in Saudi. The Wahhabis aren't too thrilled about MBS's liberalization efforts and the Saudi economy is in the pits and will stay there unless oil busts eighty dollars a barrel."

"Where's Jordan in all of this?"

"We informed them of the situation and they've pledged to support the Saudis."

"This would be a good time for the UAE and Saudi to spread some money around."

"That's exactly what they're doing."

"What about me? What do you need from Trident?"

"I need you to start working on a plan to take the artifacts back from the Brotherhood."

"You said Hamas has them in Israel."

"Yeah, that's it. We don't know much more than that."

CHAPTER 10

London

Prince Turki looked out at the green expanse of Hyde Park from the balcony of his Kensington mansion. It was a bright, sunny spring morning with the Park lawn a lush green and the trees and flowers in full bloom. The London commuters were out in force enjoying a respite from what had been a record-setting cold and snowy winter. Despite the warmth of the sun, a cold chill ran down his spine, as he couldn't shake the memory of lying on the floor of the deep freeze at the Ritz.

Tiffany, his regular London companion, came to him with a cup of black tea. He took the cup and saucer and laid it on the rail. The former runway and magazine model was thirty years his junior. She spoke with a perfect upper-class London accent, despite being a recent immigrant from Estonia. The statuesque blonde was one of his many expensive hobbies, but even she wouldn't be able to distract him on this day.

"You have a visitor. He's waiting for you in the den."

"Tell him I'll be down in a moment."

The Prince drank his tea while gazing down at the pedestrians bustling on the sidewalk as they made their way to work. The sun reflecting off the Prince Albert Statue within the Park reminded him of his nemesis who was also a prince. Prince Turki finished his tea and made his way to the elevator to meet his guest on the ground floor.

Dressed casually in pants and a polo shirt, the Prince greeted his guest. A servant entered the room and he quickly dismissed him with a hand wave. He waited until the heavy oak door was closed before beginning the conversation.

"MBS is alive," Prince Turki said.

"How do you know?" replied the Egyptian.

"I have sources. Prince Mohamed Bin Salem was wounded in the attack. He's recovering in his Palace in Jedda."

"We'll make another attempt."

"No, you'll take no further action. Besides yourself, how many other people had knowledge of the attack?"

"Most of the attackers were killed during the fight. None of them can be traced to me, which means they can't be traced to you. Four of the men who took part in the attack escaped; they're all in Djibouti in hiding."

"Kill everyone who participated in the attack or who had any knowledge of the plan. Destroy all documents connecting us. If you do that, I will pay you the second half of your contract." The Egyptian was stunned. He dropped his head and wiped his brow with his hand.

"I can't. Those men are loyal, and they fought valiantly. My men were outgunned from the moment they entered the Palace grounds. It was a phenomenal achievement to even get close enough to the Crown Prince to wound him. You should be rewarding my men, not disposing of them like trash."

"Then I'll use the ten million from the second half of the contract and pay someone else to do the job and you can be sure your name will be the first on the list."

The heavy-set Egyptian wiped his brow again, this time with a napkin from the silver coffee service displayed in front of him on the coffee table. He was silent for a full minute.

"I will do as you ask."

"Forget you ever met me. Understand the stakes are very high. I have three sons, one daughter, and eleven grandchildren living inside the Kingdom. My family is being kept prisoner, denied permission to leave. If MBS even suspects I'm the one responsible for the attempt on his life, he'll retaliate. You don't want to be the person responsible for harm coming to my family."

The bald, sweat-soaked Egyptian trembled as he stood up from his chair. He extended his hand, but Prince Turki did not accept it. Hiring the former Egyptian General to exact his revenge had been a mistake. The plan had been hastily conceived, driven by emotion and rushed into execution. The General lacked creativity, relying on brute force instead of deception and stealth. He regretted ever setting the plan into motion. Now the entire security apparatus of the Saudi government was alert and focused on tracking the people who were behind the assassination attempt. Eventually, if uninterrupted, the truth would be revealed. He hoped the Saudi investigation would take months and provide enough time for his better, more elaborate and less direct plan to reach completion.

CHAPTER 11

Ankara, Turkey

Omer Aslan was sitting at the desk in his study. It was the third week of the Holy Month of Ramadan and heavy bags had formed under his eyes from a lack of sleep, thirst, and hunger. Observant to all five daily prayers, Omer had not slept more than four hours at any one time during the fasting period. Abstaining from water and food for more than fifteen hours each day had taken a toll, but at the same time, he found the experience spiritually and physically enriching. Unlike many of his gluttonous co-religionists who gain weight during the fast, his meals during Ramadan were meager and his weight loss significant.

His office was decorated with artifacts of the Ottoman Empire. He had two fifteenth-century suits of armor with the distinctive Turkish spiked helmets, chain mail, and curved scimitars of the period. Many of the artifacts were sculptures and earthenware which he displayed on wooden shelves lining two of the walls. The third wall contained a bookshelf filled with historical tomes and the fourth wall was all glass, with a sliding door that led into the courtyard of his estate. The home was made of sandstone and bore a very strong resemblance to a medieval castle, complete with towers and ramparts.

He received Prince Turki's emissary in the small sitting area next to the entertainment center. He greeted the man with a handshake.

"His Royal Highness requests a status report," said the man whose name he did not know.

"The artifacts are in Jerusalem. On the holy day of Eid Al Fitr, there will be a groundswell of imams across the Muslim world, both Sunna and Shia, who will proclaim the Qibla as Jerusalem."

"How many imams?"

"Thousands, including many of the most influential Islamic scholars."

"How can you be sure?"

"We have brought the message to the people and it has been well received. My sources are reliable. The liberalization actions of the Saudi Crown Prince are an insult to Islam, abhorrent to many. The clarity of the revelation and authenticity of the book cannot be contested. Those three factors have proved to be very convincing. Members of our movement have been involved with lengthy discussions with the faithful. We have received assurances."

"All Salafists?"

"Not all, but many."

"What of the Shia?"

"About the same."

"Do we retain the element of surprise?"

"Our task required us to provide the information to hundreds of Brotherhood scholars who then engaged in lengthy debate before deciding to assist. Those scholars became our agents, who then went out and brought the news to thousands of imams across the globe. Not all who heard the truth were convinced. It was only a matter of time before the Saudi Intelligence Service and the Western governments who depend on Saudi oil learned of the plan."

"Has there been a counter effort?"

"Yes, of course."

"The Saudis and Emirates are trying to buy loyalty. But it's too little too late; the faithful have lost confidence in the house of Saud as the protector of the faith. They believe the liberalization movement sponsored by the Saudi Crown Prince is a betrayal of the teachings of the Prophet. MBS has become a symbol of decadence and corruption, especially with his five hundred-million-euro French Palace, five hundred-million-euro yacht, and five hundred million-euro Da Vinci painting of a nude woman that hangs in the Museum in Abu Dhabi."

"Is that all?"

"No, there's also a faction within the Islamic community who reject the book and consider it heresy. They believe, as they were always taught, that there was never but one version of the Holy Book and they view this revelation as a hoax fabricated by enemies of Islam."

"What enemies?"

"It varies. Some say the Zionists: others claim the Persians, and still others blame Rome. What's important is that all throughout Islam the few thousands who have been made aware of the book have taken sides. When over one billion of the faithful hear the news, they will do the same. All will choose a side."

"And what will happen next?"

"Holy War; the different sides will fight!"

"And this is what we want?"

"We don't want this war. We accept that it must happen; it is Allah's will. We must remove the weeds from the garden. What MBS has begun cannot be tolerated."

"What of Israel?"

"When the news is revealed, it will elevate Jerusalem to the most important place in the Muslim world. The Qibla cannot remain under Zionist control. The news will usher in change."

"Do you see any threats to the plan?"

"No. It's too late to stop it. Many thousands will speak— too many to block them all. On Friday, June fifteenth, the truth will be unveiled, and the world will change."

"What of the book and the stone?"

"Both will be displayed in Al-Masjid Mosque, and woe unto the man who attempts to remove them."

Chapter 12

Jerusalem, Israel

As I walked out from baggage claim and entered the lobby, I saw a man holding a sign with my name on it. He took my bag and I followed him onto the street. He opened the rear passenger door of a Maybach S600 limousine and I stepped in.

A man was already seated in the back seat, on the driver's side.

"Avashi, you're looking well," I said.

"Like hell, I do. I look like I'm dying."

"You've been saying that for twenty years; your wife told me that herself."

"She would know; she's the reason."

"You act like she's poisoning you."

"I wouldn't put it past her."

"Somehow, having met your wife, I don't believe that."

"It's a front. Don't let her fool you; she's the devil."

"Where are we going?"

"To the Hilton, to check you in, and then to my house for dinner."

"I thought your wife was trying to off you."

"She's a marvelous cook, and I'm sure she lays off the arsenic when we have company."

"Wow. That sounds so appealing."

"Sheila won't disappoint; she's been cooking all afternoon. For some odd reason, she likes you."

"It's a thing. Women feel sorry for me."

"And men envy you?"

"It's a conundrum."

"No, It's a paradox."

"A paradox; you're such a philosopher. Where do you find the time to be a spymaster?"

"I'm mostly retired these days. My replacement is firmly in the seat, and all I have left is the title."

"Do people in your business ever retire?"

"It's not allowed. Many of the old guard have already passed, and the rest like me continue to putter along until it's our time."

Avashi accompanied me while I checked into my hotel room. Traveling in an armored limousine with Avashi's four-man personal security detail was not exactly the low visibility profile I was looking for, but I had no choice, so I just rolled with it. My room was a suite on the club floor overlooking the Mediterranean. The beach in front of the hotel is a public one and because it's adjacent to a popular park, it's one of the most crowded in Tel-Aviv. From my ninth-floor vantage point on the balcony, looking down, the music and rowdy crowd confirmed it to be a real party spot.

Thirty minutes later we arrived at Avashi's villa. He owns a beautiful historic home in the older Lev Hair district in the center of the city. We entered through a private garden and found Sheila working in the kitchen. In complete contrast to the fair-skinned, blue-eyed Avashi, who could easily pass for a Gentile, Sheila is a Misrahi Jew, with the dark ebony skin, brown eyes and black hair of her Arab ancestors. Sheila gave me a hug. At seventy-five, she was full of life. I hadn't known Avashi long. We became acquainted when I was tasked with hunting down a group of Hezbollah operatives involved in the drug trade. At one point, we were looking for some leads and Mike referred me to Avashi who proved to be an invaluable source of information on the group's activities.

"Welcome, Pat. I'm so happy to see you!" Sheila said as she gave me a big hug.

"Thanks for having me," I said, as Sheila brushed flour off my dark blue polo shirt.

"I'm sorry, let me get a cloth."

"It's OK," I said.

"Come, let's talk. Dear, we'll be down when dinner is ready."

I followed Avashi upstairs to his office. The home was built in 1929 and is one of the oldest in the city. It was a classic home, very tastefully decorated in modern contemporary décor. On the stairwell were pictures of Avashi's only son, looking sharp, dressed in his Air Force uniform. Mike told me Avashi's son was killed in the Dizengoff bombing in 1994. I had to look up the attack as there have been so many in Israel over the years, I learned Hamas killed Avashi's son and nineteen others only three city blocks from this home.

The office was cluttered with books and still had an old electric typewriter sitting on the desk. The room was dark because, in true spymaster fashion, it didn't have any exterior windows. I sat in a heavy leather recliner. Avashi handed me a wine glass and then went to a cabinet and retrieved a bottle of red wine. He opened the wine expertly on his desk with a waiter's corkscrew.

"This a 2012 Psagot Cabernet Sauvignon from Judean Hills. Tell me what you think," he said, while filling my glass. I swirled it around in my glass and gave it a sniff before tasting it.

"It's very good. I didn't know Israel made quality wine."

"Until just a few years ago, we didn't. But now all that is changing. We have several excellent vineyards, especially in the Psagot region."

"Maybe you should join the movement, put an end to city life, move out into the country and work the fields picking grapes."

"When I first came to Israel, I worked on a farm. I was a member of a Kibbutz. We grew many things, mostly vegetables. I did my share of vegetable picking. That's where I met Sheila."

"How long ago was that?"

"That was in 1957."

"When did you get into the spy business?"

"Back then, I did both. The Mossad was in its early days. The settlements were the wild west, lots of threats, much to do."

I was comfortable and looking forward to hearing Avashi reminisce. His stories are fascinating. Compared to Avashi, my life has been boring, which for some reason is something I've always found comforting. Kind of like the Chinese curse, "May you live in interesting times."

"Before I travel back to memory lane, we need to discuss the purpose of your visit."

"Do you have the location of the book?"

"I do, but we've had a change of heart. I discussed this with my counterpart in the US and we both agreed, it would be best not to try to take back the artifacts."

"Why didn't Mike notify me? He could've saved me a trip."

"He's expecting your call. I told him it would be best if I explained our reasoning in person."

"OK, I'm listening."

"Knowledge of the book is widespread; thousands of imams have already been made aware of its existence. Regardless of how it happens, if the book goes missing, Israel will be blamed."

"Probably."

"If the people believe we took it, then we think it would add credibility to claims of its authenticity."

"From what I heard from the person who found it and studied it, the book is authentic."

"That may be so, but the millions, the hundreds of millions of people it will affect, will never see the book. Most couldn't read it even if they did. The best way to minimize the damage to Israel and to the Muslim world is to discredit the book, not to validate it by taking it seriously enough to capture."

"How do you do that?"

"With a propaganda campaign. This is something we know how to do. It has already begun."

"So, I came all the way out here for nothing?"

"Not for nothing. We have this wonderful wine, and Sheila is cooking us a lamb dinner. You're in Tel Aviv on a beautiful summer evening, with wonderful nightlife. Enjoy the moment, Pat."

After dinner, I called Mike, and he confirmed the change in mission. I returned to the dining room table for coffee. Sheila was in the kitchen. Despite her age, the woman never sat still. She was constantly doting on Avashi.

"Did you talk to Mike?"

"Yes, he confirmed what you already told me."

"You didn't come out here for nothing. I needed for you to have already spoken to Mike before sharing with you this next bit of information."

"Why?"

"You can figure that out for yourself."

"OK, I'm officially waiting for the shoe to drop."

"The second part of your mission is Omer Aslan, yes?"

"Yeah, job one was the artifacts and taking out Omer is job two."

"Omer is hired help. He's working for someone else, the big fish."

"Let me guess; you're asking for a change of mission on job two."

"Exactly. Omer is an empty target; there's no payoff. He's a bad guy, but he's already finished his role by putting everything in motion. He's not the man calling the shots; taking him out isn't going to change a thing."

"What about his boss?"

"We need to find out who he's working for, which means we need to keep Omer in play until we can figure that out."

"It will be easier if we just ask Omer. I can be very persuasive."

"If you were to capture Omer, his network would shut down. It's the wrong answer."

"What's the right answer?"

"Surveillance."

"Why are you telling me this? It's a conversation you should be having with the top guys in the Agency; I'm just a contractor, hired help."

"When I broached the subject, your friend Mike and the Deputy Director of Operations both refused to even acknowledge Omer was on the target list."

"So, you decided to take advantage of my inability to keep a secret," I said as Avashi grinned.

"No, I decided to take advantage of our relationship and ask you to talk to Mike on the subject."

"How big a problem will this reorientation of the Qibla be to Israel anyway? Jerusalem has always been a holy place for the Muslims and is already a source of violence and conflict as a result. What's going to change?"

"The Dome of the Rock was built where Muslims believe Mohammed ascended into heaven. They also believe it's the same spot Mohammed received the second pillar of Islam."

"On the night ride."

"The Quran doesn't even mention Jerusalem when it references the night ride. It says only that Mohammed rode a steed in a single night to the farthest Mosque. It was a Hadith written by Majid, who was a young boy at the time, that references Jerusalem as the place of the farthest Mosque, despite the fact that no such building existed at the time."

"The importance of Jerusalem to Islam is based on a young boy's story, a flying horse, and a non-existing building?"

"That, my friend, is why it's called faith."

"That information is already universally known. Jerusalem was the first Qibla, which at the time was a Christian stronghold. What difference will it make if Jerusalem is the Qibla again while it's a Jewish stronghold?"

"You don't have to be a scholar to understand that it didn't work out all that well for the Christians. We don't expect it will be any different this time for the Jews."

"That's been tried a few times since Israel was created. I don't see the outcome changing if any if those guys get too worked up about an old book."

"Except for Iran, none of the other nations are calling for the destruction of Israel these days. It's mostly non-state actors using *death to Israel* as a rally call. Most of the countries in the region are too focused on other threats. They have enough on their plate worrying about each other and can't be bothered with Israel."

"Do you think the announcement about the new Qibla will change that?"

"It could. Many of the dictators and monarchs in the region are hanging on to control by a thread; they'll adjust policy to conform to the wishes of the people."

"That's hard to believe."

"Not really. In 1979, Saudi Arabia was a far more moderate and tolerant society than it is today. But after Mecca was seized by religious extremists who were protesting against Saudi liberalism, King Khalid implemented a much stricter Sharia Law and gave over a lot of control to the religious authorities."

"You think the same thing could happen now."

"If the situation is improperly handled, yes. It's possible that many of the Arab nations who've improved relations with Israel in recent years will find themselves having to dial it back and take a much stronger stance against us."

"No matter what, the announcement is going to be a destabilizing influence in the region."

"It will, and taking out Omer is not going to change that. We need to find out who's behind this and deal with him or them."

"What do you want me to do?"

"Talk to Mike about the Omer op, see if you can't change the Agency's mind on a course of action that will only make our work harder."

"I'll give it a shot."

"He listens to you more than you know."

"What I hate about working with spooks is that you're always listening to me, mostly without my knowledge or consent." Avashi laughed and finished his coffee, which I took as my cue to leave.

I said farewell to Sheila and Avashi and went for a stroll. My hotel was located only half a mile away and I felt like a walk. When I passed I small café on Levontin Street at the halfway point, I heard live music coming from within. I decided to check it out. Above the door was a sign, *Levontin 7*. I opened the glass door and walked in. The room was dark. Inside I found a band sporting 1990-era heavy metal haircuts, pounding out Nirvana. A shirtless, heavily-tatted drummer was the lead singer. I sat at a small table against the wall and ordered a Tuborg Red draft beer from the waitress.

It was as good a place as any to think. I was unsure of what my next move should be. After two sets of heavy metal and five beers, an idea was beginning to form. I decided that Turkey was going to be my next destination. Omer was in Turkey and that was where Mike would expect me to go. I would request he meet me there to discuss the plan and then I'd share with him Avashi's point of view. If Mike agreed, then he would use surveillance assets from within the Agency. He wouldn't use Trident, because that's not our strong suit. We are much better suited for kinetic actions.

CHAPTER 13

Istanbul, Turkey

I met Mike at Spago Restaurant at the St. Regis Hotel in Istanbul. It was a hot summer night, made comfortable by a steady breeze blowing through the rooftop eatery. We were seated at a table with a beautiful view overlooking the Bosporus.

The waiter handed us menus written in Turkish and Italian. Mike looked at his in disbelief.

"What am I supposed to do with this?" he asked while holding his menu out in front of him.

"Look for the key Italian words; pollo, parmigiana, Chianti, stuff like that." Mike went back to staring at the menu.

"That's not going to work."

"It's Italian food; just tell the waiter what you like and let him figure it out. Four pastas, four meats, and two sauces make up ninety percent of what's on an Italian menu. Pick a combo that you like and let the waiter do the rest."

"I remember when the Turks used to be a lot friendlier about simple things like giving American guests English menus."

"Next time we pick sides in a coup d'état, maybe we should make sure we pick the winning side. But then again, I guess that explains why all those intel geniuses at CIA headquarters are still working because if they knew how to pick winners they'd have all made millions at the track."

"I've heard that argument before; it makes no sense."

"You're right. But still, the Turkish coup was a big mistake."

"It was a serious mess, that's for sure."

"It wasn't on your watch, was it?"

"No, Turkey isn't part of my area; it falls under a different section."

"Is that guy still employed?"

"No, he got hit by the perfect trifecta— Crimea, Ukraine and Turkey. The last three years of the previous administration were kind of rough on the Central Asian Desk."

"I'll bet."

"When I took over the Middle East in 2014, I had no place to go but up. Seriously, things were that bad after Arab Spring."

"Timing is everything."

"It is. Which reminds me that it's time for food."

"What do you feel like? Steak? Chicken? Veal? Fish? I'll tell you what, let me surprise you."

I muddled through the order for both of us. I even managed to find a bottle of Tuscan red, a Solaia 2013 that showed great promise, according to the Vivino wine app I checked on my cell phone.

We finished our meal, left the St. Regis, and walked six blocks to the Divine Brasserie and Jazz Club, still in the Nisantasi District. It was hot, and by the time we reached the bar, we had worked up a thirst. It was dark downstairs in the club area. We were given a seat against the wall, not far from the five-person band. The music was loud, so it was a good place to talk shop. We both ordered a draft beer.

I relayed the conversation I had with Avashi. To compensate for the music, our heads were almost touching. When I finished, Mike sat back in his chair. We listened to the rest of the set without conversation. The band was very skilled. The lead singer was a tall, dark-haired Turkish beauty in a black evening gown who did a pretty fair Billie Holiday imitation.

"Avashi wants Omer off the target list," Mike said.

"He wants his guys to surveil instead."

"And then what?"

"After the announcement of the Qibla is made and all hell breaks loose, we find who hired Omer and target them."

"Just because somebody is providing funding to Omer doesn't make him the head of the snake. Omer could be pursuing his own agenda and be receiving funding from someone with a similar aim."

"Either way, we wait and then we roll up Omer and whoever his backers are."

"Because it's already too late to stop the chaos."

"That's Avashi's viewpoint."

"What's your plan?"

"I was going to hang out in Istanbul and see what kind of chaos a thirteen-hundred-year-old book can create."

"I need to fly back tomorrow morning; otherwise I'd join you."

"In the meantime, I suggest we drink heavily, for the end is near."

I woke the next morning with a bit of a hangover. I had a suite at the St. Regis, and I heard a noise outside my door. I assumed it was the butler setting up for breakfast. I grabbed the bathrobe at the base of the bed and walked out into the living room. I was barely a step out of the room when Cheryl wrapped her arms around me. I hugged her back.

"You don't look so good. What did you do last night?" asked Cheryl.

"Mike and I went on a bit of a bender."

"What was the occasion?"

"End of the world party."

"Not funny. Take a shower; I'll order breakfast."

"Just hit the buzzer and ask for Bader."

"Who's Bader?"

"My personal butler."

"Seriously?"

"He came with the room. Like a house elf. He needs work, but I never have anything for him to do. I'm too low maintenance. I think he feels insulted that I don't ask him to do stuff."

"Walsh problems are unique to only you."

"Just order breakfast while I make myself presentable."

We ate breakfast in the dining area. Eggs Benedict and bacon did wonders for my condition. Cheryl had fruit, yogurt, and tea.

"What a view," she said while looking out at the Bosporus and the Asian side of Istanbul beyond.

"I never get tired of this view. Imagine what it was like during the Crusades when the Templars landed to lay siege to Constantinople."

"Did they land here?"

"Yeah, I think so. We should go to Old Town and check out the palaces, museums, the Hagia Sophia, and the rest of the sights."

"Let's do that in the afternoon. I didn't sleep well on the plane; I could use a nap." She said with a sly smile. I gulped and took her by the hand and led her toward the bedroom. On the way, I asked Bader to reserve a car for the afternoon. Filled with purpose, he finished clearing the table and left like a man on a mission.

I woke up from a short nap and turned on the television. Sitting up in bed, I turned on CNN. The lead story was a violent Palestinian protest in Gaza. The grievance was Jerusalem and the restricted access for the Palestinians imposed by the Israelis. Flicking between BBC, CNN, and Al Jazeera, the picture became clear; the Muslim world was once again in a state of heightened unrest. Reports of protests in Iran were the most concerning. Because of the media restrictions, the footage was not nearly as dramatic as in Palestine and Egypt, but based on my conversations with Mike, I was sure they would be the protests with the most far-reaching consequences.

Cheryl was curled up next to me sleeping. I was anxious to go outside and see the reaction of the Istanbul citizens to the revelations announced by their local imams about the lost Koran and the Qibla. It was past two in the afternoon; prayer and the weekly holy day Friday lectures from the imams should have all been finished by now. I decided to stick to the TV and let Cheryl sleep in for a while. Watching the world news would let me gauge the reaction as word swept east from time zone to time zone.

It was nearly six when Cheryl woke up and got out of bed. She dressed, and we went out for a walk. It was a beautiful weekend summer day in Istanbul. The St. Regis is bordered by Macka Park on one side and by the upscale Nisantasi district shopping area on the other. We had an eight o'clock seating at Nicole's for dinner. Nicole's is my favorite restaurant in Istanbul and is located on an office building rooftop in the Taksim area. We had skipped lunch and I was really looking forward to whatever Chef Nicole had planned for tonight's twelve-course set menu. I took Cheryl's hand as we exited the hotel. We were both dressed for dinner. She was wearing a floral summer dress and sandals, and I was wearing jeans, loafers and a black button-down shirt.

We walked south along the beautifully manicured, tree-lined trails of Macka Park. As we approached the southern exit, we heard sounds of protest coming from the vicinity of Taksim Square. We stopped at the Macka Park exit gate to get our bearings. The protests didn't sound much different from the many I'd seen over the years at Taksim. From our vantage point, looking south we could see the Dolmabahce Clock Tower and beyond that, the blue waters of the Bosporos. To our west was Vodafone Sports Stadium and hidden behind it to the west was Taksim Square. Farther to the east, out of our view, was the Dolmabahce Mosque.

The police presence intensified as we came nearer to Taksim Square. Once we reached the boundary of the Square, there were hundreds of police decked out in full riot control gear with shields and helmets. There was a cacophony of megaphone-amplified rally speakers shouting over each other in Turkish. The square was packed with thousands of people. The crowd was a mixture of young and old, although mostly young. Cheryl and I didn't enter the Square; protests are common in Istanbul and the Taksim is almost always the center for them. Democracy and the frequent military coups have always made for a tumultuous government in Turkey and this Qibla-inspired protest didn't look much different from what I had witnessed in the past.

"Let's head back and grab a taxi to the restaurant," Cheryl said.

"OK," I said. We both turned away from the crowd, and before I could take a single step, I heard a loud whack and saw Cheryl in my periphery sprawl forward onto the sidewalk face first. I dropped my head and raised my left arm as I turned to my left. I felt the sting of a club against my upper back and my left arm went temporarily numb. I dropped to one knee as a stinging pain shot down my spine and watched another man with a raised club step forward to deliver another blow. I sprang at the man at a speed he couldn't comprehend and definitely didn't expect. I felt his jaw shatter like glass from the impact of my right fist. The mob descended on me from every direction. It was impossible to isolate a single target as the men came at me fast and hard; it was a blur. Clubs, fists, and kicks rained onto me. I countered in a whirling dervish of blows of my own.

For every strike I gave, I took three in return. The big difference is that I can take a punch, and when I connect with a hit, it's a game ender for the poor son of a bitch on the receiving end. It felt like an eternity, but in a matter of minutes, the swarming mob backed away. I was out of breath and exhausted as I took stock of the situation. Five men were unconscious and unmoving on the ground. Another three were down, crying out in pain. At least two had their femurs snapped with straight kicks. I walked over to Cheryl who was lying unconscious on the sidewalk and I threw her over my still-tingling left shoulder. I picked up a stray Billy club and held it at the ready in my right hand. A new crowd of angry Turks was forming all around us. For the time being, they maintained their distance. The police were nowhere to be found.

Cheryl began to stir. I let her down and held her by the waist.

"Can you walk?" I asked.

"Yes, I'm OK," she said, as she gingerly bent down and picked up two sticks no longer used by our assailants.

"I'll clear a path through the crowd. Stay close behind me," I said.

"I'm with you," Cheryl replied.

My face and shirt were covered in blood. I could see fear in the eyes of the crowd in front of me, but I could also see anger. The sight of my six foot five, 220 pounds in full bloodlust would have been enough to cause any rational man to back down. Unfortunately, the psychology of the mob always leads to false bravado, and this case was no different.

The first attacker made his move and came at me from the front with a club raised in his hand. I cracked his skull open with a brutal overhand stroke of my baton. Fists and clubs rained down on me from both sides. I advanced forward through the assault and snapped the leg of the next Turkish man in front of me with a straight right kick. I followed the kick with a right forehand sweep of the club that shattered the teeth of a Turk who nearly took my head off with a swinging club strike of his own. I used the baton as a spear and drove it into the throat of a man to my right who connected with a solid punch to my jaw. I continued the same combination of overhand, kick, sweep, and spear several more times. I could feel Cheryl struggling behind me.

My heart was pumping a mile a minute, and I was beginning to slow from fatigue. I wasn't going to last much longer. My arms were burning, but I could see daylight through the crowd. I dropped the last two Turks in front of me and turned around to check on Cheryl. She was holding the two batons nunchuk style. Blood was covering her face from the hit she had taken on the head that started the conflict. The crowd didn't follow us as we crossed the street and headed toward the Vodafone stadium. Police sirens and amplified protest speeches filled the air. I tried to hail two taxis, but neither would stop. Cheryl and I were a frightening sight.

We entered the park and moved north toward our hotel on the same trail we had started on. We found a public restroom next to the fountains and we both went into the men's room and cleaned up as best we could. Still carrying the nightsticks, we wiped them down and left them in the trash. The bleeding from the cut on top of Cheryl's head had slowed. She held a wad of paper napkins against it as we returned to the park trail to finish our trek back to the hotel.

Despite our attempt to clean up earlier, we both looked like we had just gone a couple of rounds with Muhammad Ali. When we reached the hotel, we found security guarding the entrances to the lobby. They checked our names against the list of guests and ushered us inside. Two men were seated in the lobby holding towels to their faces. Cheryl and I were not the only guests who had run afoul of the agitated locals.

One of the managers intercepted us on the way to the elevator.

"Do you need help?" he asked.

"Yes, please send the hotel doctor to our room; she's going to need stitches," I said.

Inside our suite, Badar immediately got us some ice. Cheryl went to the shower and returned to the living area wearing a hotel bathrobe and holding a damp towel against her head. I went into the shower and returned feeling fresh and clean. Except for a small bruise on the right cheek and huge welt on my left shoulder, as luck would have it, I was barely injured. Cheryl, on the other hand, looked terrible. Both of her eyes were bruised and puffy, and she was looking through narrow slits. She had a swollen lip and a big scrape on her cheekbone where she fell against the concrete sidewalk. On top of her head, she had a deep cut that was going to take a few stitches to close. Her delicate five-foot-seven-inch, 110-pound frame was battered and bruised everywhere.

We both sat on the couch waiting for the house doctor to arrive. I called my charter service and requested a plane for an immediate flight to Germany. The earliest we could fly out would be six the next morning. I arranged for a limo to pick us up at the hotel at four.

"Do you think it's safe to stay here tonight?" I asked Cheryl.

"Why wouldn't it be?" she asked.

"I'm worried about the police. Our little rumble had to have resulted in some fatalities."

"You think so?"

"I know so. At least three, probably more."

"You fight like a barbarian."

"Bad idea to hit my girl."

"We're lucky to be alive. They were worked up to a frenzy."

"About what, exactly? What did the imams say after the afternoon prayer that would have caused them to attack us? I thought the enemy would be the Saudis or the Israelis."

"Turkey has been on a heavy populist path lately, ever since Erdogan. Somehow, the shifting of the Qibla has stoked those flames even higher."

"Saudi and UAE have had a travel warning in Turkey for the past several weeks because of a number of harassing incidents. US citizens have been detained and harassed by the police ever since we backed the wrong horse during the coup a few months ago. I guess today's message was to stop with the soft stuff and get tough with the infidels."

"Hopefully, the police will be too preoccupied with the protests to chase us down."

"I'm sure they will be. But one of the things that struck me was how the police did nothing while we were being attacked."

"Yeah, it was pretty obvious whose side they were on. But even if they have been given direction to let the mobs kill the foreigners, they'll still be kept busy protecting property. Mobs get out of control easily."

The doctor came and stitched up Cheryl. He didn't give her any painkillers beyond a local anesthetic because he said she had a mild concussion. He didn't ask what happened; he had no doubt already treated other hotel guests and the news across the city made it too obvious.

We fell asleep watching the news. There were reports of riots from every country in the Middle East. The government-controlled news service in Saudi kept the details of the unrest to a minimum.

We flew out the next morning on a Gulfstream G5. It was more airplane than we needed, but I accepted it because it was the first one available.

CHAPTER 14

Riyadh, Saudi Arabia

A group of slightly more than a hundred protestors arrived and began to mill around soon after evening prayer. They started to collect on the sidewalk but soon spilled over into the streets and before long blocked traffic at the intersection of King Saud and King Fahad streets. By ten in the evening, the crowd had swelled to more than twenty thousand. In a country where protest is illegal and has historically been met with deadly gunfire from the government, the size of this demonstration was unprecedented. A phalanx of police officers in riot control gear formed a line ten deep across King Saud Street blocking the way to the huge Ministry of Interior complex that was only two hundred yards from the assembled crowd.

The protestors were all men; they sported heavy beards, wore local dress, and many carried prayer beads in their hands. These men were religious conservatives—Wahhabis. The last protests in the Kingdom took place during the Arab Spring in 2011. At the time, many of those protestors were gunned down by police for seeking increased liberalization and democracy. Today's crowd had an opposite agenda; they were protesting liberalization. The kingdom was changing; women were being allowed to drive and to leave the home unescorted. Cinemas, previously illegal, were sprouting up in malls and contaminating the people with Western culture. The religious police, the Mutawa, were being restrained. They were prohibited from making arrests and discouraged from wielding the stick against inappropriate behavior. The crowd was most incensed by the blasphemy of a second version of the Holy Quran and the attempts by their co-religionists to move the Qibla. These were all signs that it was time for action. All across the Kingdom, the faithful were assembling in protest for what had been promoted in the mosques as a Day of Rage.

Imams took turns inciting the crowd using the speaker system from the closest neighborhood mosque, which was located across the street from the King Saud Conference Center. It was almost midnight when two of the cars parked on the street in front of the Mosque exploded. The blast from the car bombs killed dozens and wounded many more. Constrained by buildings on both sides of the street, the blasts had a disastrous effect on the crowd. The location of the blast and the instinctive reaction of the crowd to flee the mayhem funneled the protestors toward the Ministry of Interior complex.

The sound of the two explosions that were seconds apart stunned the police commander. The sight of the panicked crowd stampeding toward the phalanx of police officers guarding the gates of the MOI terrified him. Without hesitation, he keyed his radio and issued the order to fire. By the time his command reached the rank and file, the running crowd had already breached the first line of police holding riot control shields. A melee ensued. Trapped between the wall surrounding the MOI building and the rushing crowd, the terrified back rows of the police line fired indiscriminately into the intermingled mass of police and protestors.

The stampede of Wahhabis didn't slow until the pile of dead bodies grew so high it formed a wall. Eventually, the human wall blocked the flow of protesters and directed them away from the police line and back down the street toward the mosque and the exploded cars. The frightened and confused surviving protesters then melted into the side streets. In their wake, they left hundreds dead and thousands wounded. The street was littered with blood-spattered white-kandura-clad Wahhabi bodies and khaki-uniformed police.

The Saudi government immediately shut down all communications, including all cell service and the internet. The story was too big and had too many witnesses to suppress. Person-to-person communications were all it took for word to get out that the government was slaughtering the religious. Among the Wahhabi community, there was only one response to the atrocity: Jihad. Saudi Arabia was at war with itself.

CHAPTER 15

London, UK

Prince Turki bin Talal Abdulaziz met his guest in his estate office in London. He sat across from Mustafa Abbas, his Lebanese attorney and fixer. The two men were drinking tea at the coffee table next to the window. Prince Turki, a germaphobe, who disdained eye contact with subordinates, ignored Mustafa, and gazed at the raindrops as they pelted the outside window.

"What news do you have of my children? I'm unable to contact anyone in Saudi," the Prince asked.

"Plans are in motion to get them out. The National Security detail that was watching them has been re-tasked because of the crisis. The MOI, Special Forces, National Guard, and the Army are all fully engaged in security operations. We're going to smuggle them out in a helicopter to a waiting yacht."

"Will that be safe?"

"Yes, the aircraft will be cleared to an offshore oil rig. It will be a minor route diversion; nobody will notice."

"When will this happen?"

"Tomorrow."

"What's the situation inside the Kingdom?"

"Chaos. The plan worked better than expected."

"Will the King retain power?"

"For now, but the only way he's going to quell the demands of the people will be to stop with the reforms. He may even need to appoint a new Crown Prince."

"Is that a possibility?"

"Yes, although so far it has only been discussed."

"Keep me informed on the movement of my children."

Realizing he was being dismissed, Abbas stood and led himself out of the room. The Prince did not even bid him farewell, much less shake his hand. Here he was saving the man's family and he was not even given the courtesy of a goodbye. He was summoned and dismissed like a dog. Abbas had been working for the Prince for over twenty years. He'd been a faithful servant for all of that time, though—he had to admit—less out of loyalty and more because the Prince paid well; Abbas had a big family and an expensive lifestyle. The economy in Lebanon had been horrible for too long, and without the patronage of the Prince, his prospects were bleak.

Being entrusted to convey the money and the message to the Prince's operatives in Saudi who planted the car bombs had changed things. Having advance knowledge of a huge upheaval in Saudi Arabia that was destined to cause a huge spike in oil prices presented a once-in-a-lifetime opportunity for Abbas. After considering the economic impact of the plot the Prince was hatching, he developed his own plan. He borrowed against every asset he had and put it all in a long position in the oil futures market.

Following the massacre last night in Riyadh, the price of oil had already risen twenty percent. Martial law, widespread protests, and riots were going to shut down the Saudi economy even further and drive the prices even higher. Before the crisis was over, he was betting oil prices would more than double. Abbas was only days away from becoming a very wealthy man. His involvement in the plot to destabilize the Saudi government and create a diversion to rescue the Prince's children was the greatest opportunity of his lifetime. Despite the boorish treatment from the Prince, he walked out of the stately mansion into the grey skies and London rain in a bright and cheery mood.

CHAPTER 16

Eleuthera, Bahamas

After a thorough exam in a German hospital, I booked another charter and flew Cheryl to Eleuthera, Bahamas. I have a beach house near Governors Harbor, and I thought it would be the ideal place for Cheryl to recover from her injuries.

"I think you want to spirit me away to a desolate island because you don't want people to look at me and mistake you for a woman beater."

"Only a few days ago I was being accused of being a child beater. Accusations of smacking you around would be a step up for me."

"This has been a rough assignment," she said with exasperation.

"It has, because there's no handle, just a lot of smoke with nothing we can grab onto to fix things."

"And your solution is to hide away in your lair."

"We rescued the lady Doctor. The missions to recover the book and take out Omer were aborted, which leaves us with nothing to do. It's rest and recover until something breaks. This is the best place for rest and recovery."

"You make a good point."

"Of course I do."

"Now what?"

"Now I go surfing and you rest."

I changed into my 2mm body glove wetsuit and went out to the garage and picked out a surfboard. I walked out toward the beach, past the pool and the two guesthouses. Once I got past the line of palms, I stepped onto the soft sand of the beach. The beach in this part of Eleuthera is a dusty pink; it's the most beautiful sand in the world. The conditions were excellent for early August, with swells six feet high and thirteen seconds apart. I jumped into the water and worked my way out past the break.

I'd been out splashing around in the surf for more than three hours. The sun was beginning to set when I decided to take my last run. The waves had been slowly increasing in size as the tide came in. I sat on my board looking east in search of my next ride. The sun was low and reflected orange against the turquoise-blue Bahamian waters. I waited until the swell was almost on me, and then darted toward the shore, paddling furiously. I felt the board lift and begin to drop. I popped up into a standing position, left foot forward, and rode the fall. I banked left away from the break, extended my left hand, and felt the wall of water as it curled around me as I channeled through the tube. I could feel the water closing in on me, and I turned hard left away from the beach to jump the wave and escape the wall of surf that was crashing down all around me. Not my brightest idea, because all that accomplished was to flip me upside down. The force of the wave spiked me straight down into the water. My head bounced against the soft sand below the surface before the remaining power of the surf tossed me around like I was in a washing machine.

Eventually, I surfaced and pulled the leash attached to my right leg and retrieved my board. I climbed on and paddled toward the shore. When I reached the soft pinks sands of the beach, I walked unsteadily toward the house trying to find my equilibrium. It was dark by the time I entered the house through the back deck. Cheryl was sitting with Maria at the table. Maria is a Filipina woman who looks after the house, along with her husband, Jonah.

"We were wondering if you were ever coming back," commented Cheryl.

"The conditions are amazing for this time of year, so I took full advantage of it."

"I can see that; you're staggering from exhaustion."

"I'm tired, I'm hungry, and I need a legitimate reason to stagger. But first, a shower."

"I told Maria we would walk next door to Tippy's for dinner."

"Did you forget that I was keeping you under wraps until you no longer posed a threat of getting me arrested for domestic assault?"

"I want to go out, Pat. I'm feeling caged."

"OK, then how about we take the Priest? He's good conversation and I can use him for cover."

"I haven't seen Father Tellez all day."

"I'll find him. He's probably still mourning Colombia's World Cup showing."

"That was weeks ago."

"He used to play for the National Team. Soccer people are very sensitive about such things."

The three of us got a table next door at the restaurant. Tippy's is perhaps the only beach bar in the world that insists on table reservations. It's always packed, even offseason. It was a Saturday night, they had a band playing live, and the crowd was lively.

I ordered a Holy Mackerel Ale and a bottle of Chardonnay for Cheryl and the padre. I went with my default pasta and shrimp for the main and conch salad for an appetizer. I was so hungry and focused on the bread that I didn't pay any attention to what Cheryl and Father Tellez ordered.

"I've been following the reports in Saudi. The death toll from the violence is over ten thousand," Cheryl said.

"Yet another religious war killing the masses. Let's all hold hands and sing John Lennon's *Imagine*."

"*Imagine* is a terrible song. Really, it's not religion killing those people," Father Tellez added.

"It kind of is; the religious conservatives are fighting the moderates," I said.

"That's an oversimplification. There is more to the unrest than religion. Economics and social injustice are major factors. Although, I agree it was the shame of many of the world's Muslims rejecting Saudi and praying toward Jerusalem that set the faithful off," Cheryl added.

"Who would do that? Who would light such a match in the Middle East knowing the pain and suffering it would cause?" asked Father Tellez.

"That's what David Forrest and I are working on right now. Who would benefit from the actions that have taken place? The strife and the violence? We're looking at political and financial benefits, ways to measure them, and ways to trace them to individuals," Cheryl said.

"That seems like an impossible task. The numbers are too huge," I replied.

"This is where Dave Forrest and his supercomputer and artificial intelligence comes in. He has an incredible capacity to gather all the data and sift through it at amazing speeds," Cheryl said.

"If he's doing all the work, why did you use the collective, 'we'?" I asked.

"I identify the possible benefits and suggest ways to measure it. Dave finds ways to gather the data and analyze it. We make a good team, even thousands of miles away from each other," Cheryl said.

"I thought you and I were a team," I said.

"Now that I'm beat up and ugly, I know you don't want me anymore," Cheryl said.

"I told you that was just temporary. I'll only ignore you until you get your looks back. You know I'm not that superficial. Ask Father Tellez, he'll vouch for me."

"No, I won't vouch for Pat. He's a very bad man, the worst kind of sinner. Very shallow. You're very perceptive to realize this," Father Tellez said to Cheryl with a grin.

"In a matter of days your eyes will be un-swollen, your lips unsplit, and you'll be hot once again. I'm not worried," I said.

"And once that metamorphosis happens, you'll be happy to put up with my geeky hypothesizing on how to find the bad guy behind the madness in Saudi. But, let me guess, until then, you need to concentrate on beer and food, because you've worked up a huge appetite on the water," Cheryl said in a mocking tone. We all laughed.

"You know me too well," I said.

The next morning, I woke up alone. It was before six and Cheryl was gone. I went looking and found her in my office on the top floor of the house. She was curled up on the couch drinking coffee, watching the sunrise over the Atlantic side of the island.

"Why did you leave?" I asked.

"I had an idea," she said.

"What idea?"

"What we talked about last night. Who benefits. What if we search for people who made financial trades on commodities affected by what is going on in Saudi at the moment? Tens of thousands are being killed, and oil prices are above one hundred dollars and heading higher. What if we search for the people who demonstrated knowledge of what happened before it happened, and created positions in the futures markets to take advantage of the insider information?"

"A person would have to be pretty stupid to create this kind of chaos and then leave a financial trail from trying to benefit from the misery."

"Nobody's going to leave an obvious trail."

"There are too many exchanges in the world trading oil futures, not to mention the ETFs and other financial instruments that move up and down with the price of oil."

"I've been talking to David Forrest and he's working on it."

"Do you think this will lead somewhere?" I asked.

"Yes, I do."

"Let's go to Paphos and link up with David. Whatever he finds is probably going to take us to the Middle East or Europe. Might as well get a head start."

"Schedule a plane. I'm ready now," Cheryl said.

"You look really turned on by all of this. Beyond those hideous wounds, I can almost see my former super-hot girlfriend," I said.

"Have you always been such a Neanderthal?" Cheryl asked.

"No, believe it or not, there was I time when I couldn't even bench press 315, but then, thank God, I hit puberty."

"Hopeless," Cheryl whispered under her breath as she left the room.

CHAPTER 17

Paphos, Cyprus

We touched down at Paphos International in a charter. It only took a minute to get through passport control at the lone passenger terminal. When I stepped out of the terminal, I was blanketed by the heat and humidity Cyprus is known for in the summer. A black Suburban pulled up to the curb and Migos hopped out to grab our bags. He gave Cheryl a hug, and with uncharacteristic restraint didn't say anything about her injuries. We hopped into the vehicle for the short ride to the airport cargo area where Trident leased a hangar that was shared by Clearwater.

"We've been busy making renovations. Since you got rid of the second plane, we have a lot more room to work with. We've added a small gym, a full kitchen, and a really nice break area with a big screen, couches, a full espresso bar, and a pool table. You're gonna love it," Migos said.

"Is everyone here?" I asked.

"No, the Mali delivery is running late. They were supposed to land two hours ago but got delayed in Bamako International."

"What was the problem?" I asked.

"Refueling was late. Because of maintenance problems, only one fuel truck was working to service the entire airport."

"Mali is a disaster even by African standards. But we can't refuel before getting to Mali because we can't risk the cargo getting confiscated by another African Nation. There aren't a lot of good options in Mali's neighborhood," I said.

The Trident Hangar is huge. When I originally leased the space, I needed room for two C130s and fifty thousand square feet to store cargo away from prying eyes. Trident has only one contract and that contract is to deliver military supplies to whomever the CIA tells us to deliver them to. These are all black programs supporting US interests throughout the Middle East and Africa. We have a second hangar in Darfur Air Force Base in the United Arab Emirates. The goods we ship that come from the US and Europe needing export licenses are earmarked for UAE, and then once we deliver them to Abu Dhabi, we divert them to their final destination. What we do is highly classified, and illegal as hell. When we started, all of our supplies went to the Kurds and to other rebel groups fighting ISIS in Syria and Iraq. Now that ISIS is almost a thing of the past, we do less than half of the deliveries we did at our peak. At the moment, most of our shipments are going to Chad, Mali, Syria, and Iraq.

The big hangar doors were closed. Migos parked outside and we entered through a regular door on the side of the hangar. Migos swiped his card and placed his hand on the biometric scanner to open the heavy steel interior door. The hangar was cool and dry. The spaces for the C130 and the cargo holding area were empty. Two Little Bird helicopters were parked in the load-out area. Next to the Little Birds was a 7.5 meter rigid inflatable boat, two armored SUVs, a couple of small dune-buggy-like vehicles, and a line of steel cabinets thirty yards long filled with the latest tactical equipment on the market. The hangar in Paphos doubled as the staging area for the direct-action missions Trident was occasionally tasked to perform by the Agency.

We walked toward the back of the hangar and entered the office space that was sectioned off for Clearwater. Cheryl designed and decorated the Clearwater offices and they reflect her tastes. The lighting is dim, with lots of reds and dark rich mahogany and teak. The art is Asian, mostly landscape watercolors with a few interesting jade sculptures. The dramatic contrast between the Clearwater and Trident operations doesn't stop with the décor. It's the cerebral versus the physical. I don't have to tell you where I belong.

Migos disappeared as Cheryl and I walked into David Forrest's office. Dave is an academic, the head of the University of Edinburgh's Computer Science Department, and one of the world's leading authorities on Artificial Intelligence. I met him when he was developing an underfunded aerial reconnaissance AI joint research project between the British Government, his University, and his own private company, called GSS. Clearwater is a joint venture between Trident and GSS. Clearwater makes a sizable profit every year tracking—and sometimes finding—lost commercial shipping boats. Clearwater also serves as the intelligence element for Trident. David's computer skills and Cheryl's intelligence background have proven themselves on many occasions.

Despite his new-found wealth, David Forrest hasn't changed. He's still the disheveled, portly college professor with a cliché tweed jacket and a pipe that rarely leaves his touch. Although, he did concede to Cheryl's Asian-themed high-tech office décor. On his wall, he had installed a fake picture window with a video screen displaying a Scottish highland vista. Cheryl once told me that the only reason David spends so much time in Paphos is because, at the University in Scotland, they recently began enforcing a rule prohibiting smoking in the office. At Clearwater, he could smoke his pipe as much as he wanted. The scent of Captain Black tobacco was in the air as Cheryl and I sat down on the two chairs arrayed in front of his desk.

We went through the usual pleasantries. Cheryl then told David the story of what happened in Istanbul. I could see David was genuinely distraught at Cheryl's experience. I don't like to be reminded of the event, because I should've done a better job protecting her. When Cheryl and I got together, it was never my plan to work with her. My hope was to keep Cheryl out of the business. She's a former Chinese Army Colonel, an experienced agent who worked in Military Intelligence, and later the Chinese equivalent of the CIA—a unit so secret that nobody even knows their real name, so it's called "Chinese Intelligence." Actively working with the US Government is a great way for a former Chinese operative to paint a target on their back. This is especially true with Cheryl, because the Chinese government believes she's dead. It also opens up Trident and our CIA backers to criticism. If our security ever gets compromised or an operation ever goes terribly wrong, it's very likely a US board of inquiry will point to her as the reason. Cheryl was adamant about getting involved in Clearwater and Mike Guthrie, my CIA benefactor, approved the idea. I eventually relented and allowed Cheryl to become a part of the team. What I never expected was that she would bond so well with the equally strong-willed Professor.

The conversation shifted to the problem at hand. They planned how they were going to use Clearwater's massive computing power to sift through financial transactions. They had to make requests through Agency channels to request authorization for information controlled by the US Government Intel agencies like the National Security Agency to do some of what they planned.

"You two have a lot of work to do and I'm just getting in the way. I'm going to find the *Sam Houston* at the marina. If you need me, I'll be drinking Sam Adams, fishing, and listening to country music."

"What do you see in this man?" David asked Cheryl, in mock disbelief.

"He's very handy when I need to reach high shelves, and I find his lack of curiosity can be very calming," Cheryl said. They both laughed at my expense.

"Well, just for that I'm going to drink copious amounts of Sam Adams and play Montgomery Gentry at max volume. Call me when you figure something out."

I found the *Sam Houston* in its usual slip at the end of Kato Paphos Harbor Marina. The yacht was docked closest to the medieval castle and away from the waterfront row of restaurants and cafes which are overrun with Russian tourists during the summer. My little section of the marina is an isolated area that's a refuge for the year-rounders and Coco the Pelican who is the unofficial mascot of the Marina. Occasionally, the Russian tourists slip past the Marina security in pursuit of Coco for a photo opportunity. In recent years, getting a photo with Coco has become something of a thing on Russian social media. Recently, a drunken Russian lady took her clothes off and went viral with pictures she took with the Pelican in a series of suggestive poses. The antics of holidaying Russians are a popular topic of conversation among the locals.

I hadn't been on the *Sam Houston* since Migos and I left for Syria. I did a walk around to check the state of things. McDonald was the last person to captain her. He's retired Navy, and has more weeks behind the helm of boats than I have hours. The exterior was immaculate, everything was tied up tightly and stored securely. I entered the salon and found the same. On the way to the galley, I checked the bar and the wine cooler. This is where difficulty usually arises after my team has the run of the boat. I was surprised to see only limited damage. This can be attributed to the fact that Migos was with me and not on the boat. At the wheelhouse I checked the gauges, batteries and fuel; they were all good.

I left the boat and walked over to the Kingfisher charter shed, checked on the sea conditions, and picked up some baitfish. Then I disconnected the power and water and untied the boat. I walked up the stairs to the fly deck, and snagged a bottle of Sam Adams Summer Ale from the minifridge on the way to the helm. I started her up and steered for the marina exit. I shut the twin cat engines off when I was about two miles offshore and let the sixty-four-foot yacht drift. The sea was calm with gentle rollers. It was late afternoon on a cloudless day, with only a light wind. I set up a fishing chair on the hydraulic ramp off the stern, turned on the MLB.com replay of last night's Red Sox-Yankees game with my iPad, and cast my line into the Mediterranean.

After three hours, the baseball game was over, and it was time to return to the Marina. The final score was that I got skunked, and the Sox won 4-1 in a complete game one-hitter thrown by Rick Porcello, who was looking more and more like he did the year he won the Cy Young. I was very happy with that outcome. The empty beer bottles next to my chair may have had something to do with that.

After I finished tying up the boat, I called Cheryl to make dinner plans. She and Dave were working through the night. She told me she'd let me know when they had something actionable. Cheryl didn't want me at the office. It was beginning to look like I was going to be alone for a few days. I decided to walk over to the Kingfisher shed and meet the fishing charters as they came in to gather some intel of my own. I was going out the next day to catch some tuna and I was determined not to get skunked two days in a row. My experience with fishermen has been that they are a generous breed, sharing information freely. Which is good, because I didn't want to have to go through the trouble of a night dive to attach satellite tracking beacons onto the charter boats to find the hot spots they were going to.

I fished full time for the next three days. I was grilling a tuna steak on the fly deck when I was interrupted by the distinctive ringtone from the satphone.

"Walsh Fishing Charters," I said.

"Where are you?" asked Mike.

"I'm on the water; do you need my position?"

"I'm in the region. I'm going to be in Paphos tomorrow morning."

"We're going to have an intel briefing tomorrow morning. Cheryl said they're making headway and expect to have something to report."

"Yeah, that's why I'm coming in. Clearwater has been making frequent requests for data from the Agency. We can't release anything without knowing the reason, so we've been kept up to date. The techies in our building have been really impressed with the work Clearwater is doing."

"I don't want to take too much credit for it. It's just basic leadership. It comes naturally; it's a gift, really," I said.

"What is it you've been doing anyway?"

"Inspiring from a distance. At the moment, I'm grilling a fresh bluefin steak basted lightly with lemon and butter. I have a 1982 Pomerol that I've decanted to celebrate my historic victory over the dreaded tuna population."

"How do you live with yourself? Your battered girl is working slave hours, and you're drinking premium vino on a yacht."

"It sounds kind of bad when you put it that way."

"I'm envious, is all. The crisis is getting out of hand. I'm operating on fumes. It's worse than Arab Spring. There's a real chance the Saudi government could fall."

"I'll see you in the bat cave."

CHAPTER 18

Paphos, Cyprus

T he full team was assembled around the table in the briefing room. Mike sat at the head of the table as the senior member in attendance. McDonald, Migos, Burnia, and Jankowski were bright and alert. Mike had bags under his eyes and was on his second cup of coffee. Neither Dave nor Cheryl had made an entrance. I hadn't seen either for four days. We were all making small talk, working on a box of donuts, when David Forrest made his entrance with Cheryl in tow. Cheryl looked great. The bruising was no longer visible, and the swelling around her eyes was gone. She was wearing tight blue jeans, a white t-shirt, and ponytail. Both Cheryl and David had a buoyant, enthusiastic cheer that can only come from a big win. Since neither was susceptible to false or premature celebration, I prepared myself to be wowed.

The lights dimmed and the big wall-sized screen at the end of the table came to life. We watched a CNN summary of the calamitous conflict that had erupted in the Middle East. Footage of demonstrations in Egypt, battles in Israel and Lebanon, and riots in Saudi filled the screen.

"Clearwater has been tasked with identifying the vector that triggered the latest unrest we are seeing in the Middle East."

David then went into his full college professor mode and detailed the search process with which he engaged his supercomputer and artificial intelligence software. It was an interesting brief. What I found most surprising, was the amount of intel the US Intel agencies shared with Clearwater. As if reading my mind, Mike spoke up.

"The amount of conflict we're experiencing is way out of proportion to the discovery of a lost Quran. There's something more going on, and we've had every intel service in the US focusing on figuring out what that is. The updates from Clearwater have given us reason to believe that they had the best path to figuring this out and the DNI made the decision to open the floodgates in response to your data requests."

Cheryl then took the lead as head briefer.

"We've identified seven people who've made trades that are sufficiently out of the pattern of predictable activity that they deserve to be looked into."

"What does that mean?" Mike asked.

Cheryl touched the computer mouse and the screen filled with a photo and biographical information.

"This is Mustafa Abbas. The computer identified him as having the most atypical investment behavior. The three key indicators are when he made the investment, the size of the investment relative to the size of his investment portfolio, and his net worth. And finally, the degrees of separation between him and one of the potential targets of the Quran release.

"Abbas receives a predictive score of 83% as a vector for the following reasons. He made his investment in the London Brent Crude market two days before the public release of the Quran on Friday, June 15.

"Abbas's investment of two million, three hundred and sixty-seven thousand pounds represents one hundred percent of his investment portfolio and is eight times larger than his net worth. The futures market is very high risk because it's leveraged. Abbas lacks the ability to answer a margin call. A relatively small drop in oil prices would have canceled his contract and lost him many times more money than he's worth. He borrowed against his properties in Saudi and Lebanon to make this investment, and he maxed out his credit cards and a line of credit he had for his business with his bank. Abbas is an attorney, and he illegally drained an escrow account he manages for a client to scrape up 1.3 million of the pounds he invested in this futures position.

"The third indicator is a connection to a potential victim of the Quran's release. Abbas's legal work includes corporate clients who are owned by several prominent Saudi Arabian citizens. Foremost among these prominent citizens is Prince Turki bin Talal Abdulaziz.

"Prince Turki bin Talal Abdulaziz is one of the victims of the Saudi Crown Prince's anti-corruption crackdown. He spent several months in the Ritz in Riyadh, and he had a significant amount of his own wealth confiscated by the Saudi government. Estimates go as high as sixty billion dollars. Prince Turki sold many of his assets to settle with the Saudi government. One asset he did not sell was his stake in Twitter.

"Prince Turki owns fifteen percent of Twitter; he was one of the first investors. The connection between Turki and Twitter matters, because it helps to explain an element of this crisis that Mike alluded to, and which we were having the most trouble explaining. Why are millions of people being driven to revolution about a book most of them can't even read?

"The answer to that question is a professional, highly advanced social media campaign, the kind of campaign that could only be conducted by someone with a lot of money and inside knowledge, and perhaps even access to the root programming and algorithms of Instagram, Twitter and Facebook.

"We don't know yet who's conducting this social media campaign or even where it is coming from. At this stage, we're very confident Abbas learned of the Quran plot from his client Prince Turki. Given his perilous financial condition, we believe he sought to capitalize on what he learned from his client in the Futures Market. His original, 2.3 million-pound investment is currently valued at over 57 million pounds, and if the price of oil hits two hundred dollars— which it's on course to do—he's going to make twice that amount. Prince Turki is our new target. The Israelis believe Omer Aslan had someone behind him funding his operation. We believe that someone is Prince Turki.

"We recommend Abbas for capture and interrogation. We recommend intense surveillance of Prince Turki with the purpose of finding, and then taking down the social media campaign. We believe shutting down or, ideally, white-hatting the social media campaign will go a long way in defusing this crisis."

The lights in the room brightened.

"That concludes our briefing," Cheryl said with a stoic facial expression. I could see in her eyes that she was beaming. She and

David had accomplished an amazing feat. I smiled at her; I was very proud of my Chinese spy.

"That was definitely worth the trip. This is a major break-through," Mike said.

"Do you want us to pick up Abbas?" I asked.

"Yes, but you're going to have to get your intel support from Langley. We need Clearwater to focus on the social media angle."

"This is a first; the intel geeks are taking priority over the operators. I'm not sure if I can adjust to my newfound insignificance."

"Get used to it, Pat. You were right when you said Clearwater has capabilities we don't have in Langley. This could be a game changer. We need to retake the initiative. Capture Abbas and Omer."

"Won't that spook Prince Turki?" I said.

"I'm willing to take that risk, as we don't have the time for lengthy surveillance and collection. I'm tempted to bring Turki in, but I'm afraid he's not going to talk or help us shut the revolution-making machine down. We'll collect on Turki, and capture the other two and see if they can give us something we can use against Turki."

"OK, boss. I guess that means no fishing today."

"Where's Abbas now?" Mike asked.

"He's in London, hovering around his broker's office," Cheryl answered.

"What about Omer?"

"Ankara, Turkey," said Cheryl.

"On second thought, I'll have an Agency team pick up Abbas; we need to work friendly with our cousins. Pat, your guys will take Omer. Try to do it quietly. I know you have some pent-up hostility toward the Turkish at the moment."

"Turkey's a hostile country these days. The last thing I want is to fight my way out of it. A bloodless snatch and grab will be the goal."

"You don't need to involve Langley. We can do the targeting package from here on Omer. Most of the work is already done. We've known about him for a while. It won't take away from our efforts on the social media angle," Cheryl said.

"All right, fine. I'll leave you to it. Let me know if you need anything. I have a flight to catch."

I walked with Mike to his government jet that was parked outside the Trident hangar.

"You should up the security around the hangar," he said, as we were approaching the stairs on his ride. There's more to this than we know, and we shouldn't underestimate these guys."

"Will do."

"Clearwater is paying off."

"The Scottish professor and the Chi-com defector. Who'd have thunk it?"

"The Director wants to bring them in-house."

"I don't think either one of them will go for that."

"That's what I told him."

"Have a safe flight. I'll let you know once we have Omer in flex cuffs."

"His Grey Wolves brutally murdered that Archaeology Team in Syria. Don't underestimate him either."

"I won't."

"Any thoughts on how you'll get in and out of Ankara?"

"We do a fair amount of business with MKE and several of the other Turkish defense companies. I think we'll arrange an urgent delivery of something that doesn't require an export license and fly in with the C130 to make the pickup."

"That will allow you to arrive armed and leave with Omer?"

"Yeah, we're probably going to need to go in heavy."

"Don't get caught; we won't have the ability to do much for you if you do. Erdogan isn't working friendly with the US at the moment."

"I'll let you know if we need anything."

When I returned to the hangar everyone had dispersed from the conference room. I found Cheryl asleep in the bedroom adjacent to her office. Putting in the bedroom was a smart idea; she had planned ahead for future marathon work sessions. I crawled in beside her in the twin bed as quietly as I could, because I didn't want to wake her.

"Don't you have work to do?" she said in a sleepy voice.

"Nothing that can't wait a few minutes. I missed you."

"She turned around and hugged me. She fell back asleep in seconds."

I held her while I worked out the logistics of going to Ankara in my mind.

CHAPTER 19

Ankara, Turkey

O ur C130 touched down in Ankara's International Airport as it was getting dark. We taxied to the farthest corner of the cargo area nearest the fence-line and dropped the ramp. Bill Sachse, the loadmaster, signed for an incoming shipment of engineering barrier materials and stored it in pallets next to the aircraft. I stayed inside the aircraft and took a nap until one in the morning, when it was time to move.

It took four of us to roll the MH/6S Little Bird down the ramp. The aircraft is the size of an economy car and its big bubble cockpit gives it the shape of a giant insect. The MELB version is remotely piloted and has an array of cameras and sensors surrounding it. The Little Bird has a bench seat on both sides of the empty cockpit which are mounted above the skid to externally carry passengers. We left the dumpster-sized QUADCON aluminum shipping container with the ground control station inside the aircraft.

To fit into the airplane, the rotor wings had to be folded on top of each other. We spent a few minutes moving them into flying position and then locking them down. Sachse did the final pre-flight check on the Little Bird and then gave control of the aircraft to McDonald over the radio comms. We were in an isolated corner of the airport, but there was no guarantee security wouldn't come around. McDonald started the aircraft while the four of us—Burnia, Jankowski, Migos and I— kitted up and secured ourselves on the bench seats of the aircraft, two of us on each side.

We were all wearing GPNVG-19 night vision with the four lenses that made all of us look like aliens sitting aboard the aircraft. We were wearing black tactical uniforms, and body armor vests, helmets, and black balaclavas that covered most of our faces. The rotor blades increased speed and we lifted off. The Little Bird cleared the airport boundary fence by only twenty feet.

To avoid radar we flew at treetop level. Central Turkey is hilly and heavily wooded. We avoided the towns on the way to our destination. The flight was thirty-five minutes long at a speed of sixty knots. Halfway to the objective, Cheryl's voice came over the radio. She was looking at our objective from space.

"Two guards inside the guard shack covering the front gate. No movement outside of the main residence. Three horses are corralled outside the stable. No activity coming from the house."

The Little Bird touched down in an open field surrounded by a forest a little over a mile from the estate. The aircraft began shut-down procedure while the four of us moved into the wood line and began our infiltration of the estate. The terrain was difficult. Although there was not a lot of underbrush, there were plenty of rocks, and hills were steep. It took almost forty-five minutes to reach the eight-foot-high stone wall surrounding the estate. Migos and I moved to the wall and pulled security. I took a knee and oriented right, he did the same, only orienting to the left.

"The far side is clear," Cheryl's voice said into our headsets.

Burnia came forward to the wall and placed a lightweight titanium assault ladder against it. He climbed to the top and dropped a second ladder against the opposite side. Jankowski followed Burnia, and then Migos and I followed. The distance from the wall to the house was two hundred yards. To the right of the house were the horse corral and barn. To the left was the guest house our satellite recon identified as the barracks for the security detail. Burnia and Jankowski followed the wall toward the front gate. Migos headed to the west wing of the house. I went to the guest house and emplaced two claymore mines connected by a strand of detonating-cord fifty yards in front of the house. I aimed the anti-personnel mines at the front door. I pulled out the remote sensor from my pack; it was little more than a motion detector with a five-second delay. I set it up facing the door and moved to the estate house to link up with Migos.

When I reached the grey stone exterior of the western side of the house, Migos was still emplacing the GSM frequency jammer. The jammer would shut off all cell phone service in a three-hundred-yard radius. I used the bolt cutters from my backpack and cut the phone lines, then I opened the electric box and switched off the power to the house. Burnia and Jankowski linked up with us at the front door. Burnia worked the lock with his pick tools. Jankowski held a halogen tool in his hand, just in case there was a dead bolt. I tested the PEQ-18 laser on the DDM4 300 blackout ISR and got ready. The door swung open and we filed in quietly.

Cheryl and Dave weren't able to find plans to the house. Based on the shape and the view outside, our best guess was that Omer would locate the master bedroom on the second floor facing the picturesque lake in the back. The bedrooms on the second floor were our objective, and our goal was to get to them and capture Omer before things got loud. The estate was huge and home to Omer's entire family that included his wife, seven kids, two daughters-in-law, and three grandchildren. We definitely wanted to avoid a gunfight in the house.

Our two teams started in the center of the second floor and worked outward. It was 3:00 a.m. and everyone was fast asleep. Migos and I went left and stopped at the first door on the lake side. I turned the handle on the door and quietly entered the room. It was an open room with large bookcases and shelves along the walls. Through my white phosphorous night vision goggles, everything looked like it was on a black and white television. There was a desk and lots of art and military objects on the shelves. I made a note to come back later to gather intel, but first we needed to find Omer.

"Office, no joy," I said to Migos.

Migos led us to the next door in the corridor. He entered first; I covered the hallway. A minute later I heard Jankowski's voice.

"Jackpot."

"Bring him to the office. It's the first room Migos and I went into," I said.

Migos and I went to the office.

"Site exploitation," I said over the radio.

This time I turned on the IR light attached to the side of my helmet and began a proper search. Migos did the same. A few minutes later, Jankowski and Burnia showed up with a bound and gagged Omer. He looked like he still hadn't recovered from the Taser.

"Was he alone?" I asked.

"No, his wife was with him. We zapped her and tied her up. She's gagged and still in her bed."

I went over and kneeled next to Omer who was lying on his back, eyes wide open.

"Omer, buddy. Do you remember what you did to the people in those two villas in Homs to get the book? Well, I've bad news for you. If you don't help us find a copy of that book, the same thing is going to happen here. It's called payback."

Omer nodded. Burnia cut the flex cuffs holding his feet and pulled him to a standing position. He held on to Omer as he walked to a wall. At the wall was a painting; Burnia removed the painting, and behind it was a safe. Burnia cut the flex cuffs on Omer's hands while I shined a regular pen light onto the safe.

"Open it," I said.

Omer worked the combination, pulled the lever, and the safe opened. Before he could reach inside, Burnia smothered him and tied him back up. I aimed the flashlight into the vault and found a portable hard drive, several USBs and a stack of papers, including one envelope thick enough to hold a book. I removed them and stashed them in my backpack. Then I shut the white-light flashlight off and returned my night vision in front of my eyes.

"We're still undetected. We'll extract outside the wall and let whoever is inside this place continue to sleep. Burnia threw Omer over his shoulder and we filed down the wide staircase that led to the estate's grand entryway. We exited the same door we came in, making sure to lock it on our way out. The guardhouse had doors that opened on both sides of the exterior wall. We walked out through the guardhouse door, and had to step over the two dead bodies dropped by Burnia and Jankowski on the way in as we exited.

"McDonald, what's the status on our ride?"

"Two minutes."

Seconds later, I heard the whump whump of the tiny helicopter approach.

"Activity coming from the guest house!" I heard Migos say.

I looked through the steel bars of the front gate and saw five figures leaving from the front door of the house. The lead man was already off the front stairs of the porch, and the rest were close behind him. They had already triggered the mine sensor. Seconds later the explosion flashed white through my night vision goggles. Hundreds of lethal metal balls from the twin claymore blast instantly killed all five men and blew out every window in the front of the house.

The Little Bird touched down on the access road fifty yards from our position. We hopped on the aircraft and secured ourselves on the bench seats with retention cords. I couldn't see them, but I knew Burnia and Jankowski were holding Omer between them.

The flight back to the airport gave me a lot of idle time to worry about getting out of Turkey. The GSM Jammer only had enough battery power to last an hour. If the people alive in the house were able to use a cell phone and call the authorities before our take off, we might have a problem. They were sure to look for the helicopter at the airport. We needed to get out of Turkish airspace as fast as possible. I was sure Sachse had already loaded up the pallets and cleared us through customs. Hopefully, we could land, load the Little Bird, taxi and take off before any alerts were made.

We landed next to the tail ramp of the C130. We raced into action as soon as we touched down. Burnia dragged Omer into the C130, while the rest of us got to work breaking down rotor blades. Sachse helped, and the four of us pushed the Little Bird up the ramp and into the airplane cargo hold. The tail ramp came up before we even had the MH-6 tied down. We began to taxi as McDonald and Sachse were strapping down the helicopter.

I grabbed a headset and walked over to the last window on the side of the plane in the far back. The pilots were chatting about our location and place in the queue. We were third in line to take off. They had planes landing on the same runway and it was going to take ten minutes. The communication system was connected to Paphos via an onboard satellite link. I called Cheryl.

"Are you hearing anything from the Turks?" I asked.

"Nothing yet. We can see you in the line-up, and there's no police or military activity directed at you."

Our flight plan was to Budapest, Hungary. The distance due north to the Black Sea and to the international boundary is just under two hundred miles, which at maximum speed in our C130J was going to take us twenty-five minutes. The max speed of our Hercules is 410 knots, which is painfully slow when compared to Mach 2 for the Turkish F-16s. The air defenses along the Turkish coast were another concern. We had excellent intel on the Turkish ADA positions and our route was plotted to avoid them. We had worked out a plan with several contingencies based on when the alert went out to the Turkish Air Force to stop us. The best case was that the alert wouldn't come out.

I sat in a nylon mesh seat along the fuselage and buckled in. Jankowski handed me a can of Diet Coke and I did my best to appear calm as I waited to hear the good word from the pilots.

It didn't take long. The pitch of the four turbo-props steadily climbed as they went to full power. I checked my watch as we raced down the runway. It had been seventeen minutes waiting in the queue to take off; now we needed another twenty-five to get out of Turkish airspace. The plane climbed steadily until it leveled off at ten thousand feet.

I was on the end closest to the tail gate. Migos was sitting next to me. Sachse was next to him. Burnia, Jankowski, and Omer were seated across from us. McDonald was forward in the cockpit. Now that he had all those flight hours ferrying us around remotely in the Little Bird, he liked to think of himself as a pilot. We were all buckled in. We had the white lights on in the airplane. None of the guys were talking; everyone was straight-faced and sober.

"Turkish Air Force has issued intercept orders," Cheryl said over the intercom. I looked at my watch; we needed fourteen more minutes to reach freedom."

The plane dropped so fast it felt like my stomach was in my mouth.

Before long, we were flying one hundred feet above the ground. We were bouncing and jiggling around the terrain as we raced through the dark night. It's times like this that I appreciated the quality of the former Air Force Special Operations pilots we had on the Trident team. I knew we had the best pilots, best plane, with the best countermeasures on the market. We were going against a force equipped with NATO Air Defenses and F-16s. *If the Turks catch us, we're dead,* I thought. The two US Air Force bases are located south of Ankara, and neither would be notified by the Turks to scramble aircraft for this emergency, so the number of on-call ready interceptors available to the Turks was very limited. Our intel had it pegged to only two aircraft.

The chatter from the two pilots was steady and calm. I heard the radar alarm over my headset.

"That's a ground-based radar system, you'll outrun it in a minute," I heard Cheryl say. "Change heading to twelve degrees on my order; stand by for my go," she said.

I knew Cheryl was going to divert our course once we got out of range of the radar. She didn't want the air defenders to plot our flight path so the fighter jets could track us down.

As we were waiting to make the turn, a different alarm went off. The vibration of the countermeasures firing from the wings shook the aircraft. These weren't flares and chaff like in the old days; the aircraft had fourth generation countermeasures that can defeat both heat-seekers and radar guided missiles. Everybody on the team was wearing headsets and listening the same as I was. I don't think any of us were breathing.

A full minute went by.

"Go!" I heard Cheryl say. The plane banked steeply to the right. Everybody was frozen still for another two minutes.

"Feet wet," I heard over my headset. We were finally over the Black Sea. I looked at my watch and stared at the second hand. It swept the face once; halfway through the second rotation, I heard over the headset, "Touchdown." We had crossed over the line into international waters. We stayed low skimming the waves, but returned to our original course. We went back up to ten thousand feet before entering Romanian airspace. It was another three hours before we landed in Macedonia. We were all very happy to hand Omer and the intel we grabbed over to the CIA agent who met us at the tarmac of the airport. We refueled and then headed back to Paphos. This time when we took off, nobody buckled up; instead. we erected hammocks inside the airplane and went to sleep.

"I don't think we should be taking this airplane anywhere near Turkey in the future," Migos said from his hammock.

"We'll change the corporate ownership, the tail number; before long we'll be landing in Istanbul," I said.

"Not me. I draw the line at surface-to-air missiles. This is not the first time that has happened."

"I'll bet you won't be joking about how easy the Air Force has it for a while," Sachse said in his Kentucky twang. We all laughed at that.

CHAPTER 20

London, UK

The Prince paced in front of his office desk. He was still at his London estate where he had been ensconced since fleeing Riyadh so many months before. He nervously stroked his mustache as he paced. His approach to life had always been as if it were a game of chess. He was winning, but he had to sacrifice a few pieces along the way to get to his position. Omer and Abbas had both dropped off the map, which was worrisome. But, on the positive side, his children were again by his side, and his archenemy was about to lose his Kingdom. Saudi was on the brink of a full-scale civil war, and Turki had every intention of pushing it over the edge with his next move.

The thought of the torment he was causing his cousin made him smile. He couldn't help but think, if given the chance, MBS would gladly return his billions several times over if it would erase the last weeks of unrest that threatened his Kingdom. He had no intention of making it that easy; he wasn't going to let up until the Crown Prince fled Saudi and exiled himself at his French palace. Even that wouldn't be the end of it, because Prince Turki had yet another surprise waiting for him in France.

The disappearance of Omer wasn't his main worry. Omer had been essential early on, as he was the person who brought the lost Quran to his attention. In the beginning of the plan, Omer was very active operationally, particularly with the attack on the Shirin compound and seizure of the artifacts. It made sense that his activities would eventually be discovered. The Israelis, Americans, Saudis, or even one of the European countries whose citizens he had massacred in Homs had probably snatched him. It didn't matter. Omer had never been afforded the privilege of learning the Prince's grand design.

Abbas was a different matter altogether. His familiarity with the Prince was much greater, and there was no good reason he should have come to the attention of an intelligence agency. Which could only mean he was not aware of something important that was going on. This not knowing concerned him greatly. As a precaution, he decided to relocate to someplace where he could have heavily armed security and the support of a friendly government. Morocco was the place. He had an excellent relationship with King Mohammed and the cash-strapped former playboy was always willing to turn a blind eye in exchange for a generous donation.

He owned a beautiful estate in Tangier. He had not visited in almost a year, and he missed it. This would be the perfect time to make use of it. The home was isolated, easily defended, and would offer him the privacy he needed to stay off the grid until it was safe again to show himself.

CHAPTER 21

Paphos, Cyprus

I was in my perch on the fly deck of the *Sam Houston*, still docked at the Paphos Marina. A portable fan was gyrating on the table next to me to combat the heat. I watched Mike as he passed Coco the flamingo on his way down the narrow walkway to the marina gate. The guard let Mike pass, and he continued toward the *Sam Houston* with his distinctive limp. I waved him aboard, and he climbed up the stairs and took a seat on the couch directly opposite me. I got up and got a bottle of Sam Adams for each of us from the mini-fridge.

"I'll bet after spending most of the day with Dr. Forrest you can use a beer," I said while handing him a frosty bottle.

"He's an impressive guy. With this latest line of inquiry, Cheryl and Dave seem to have knocked over a bee's nest."

"What do you mean?"

"They're under a cyber-attack. They've been defending against a deluge of hacking attempts from an unknown source."

"Do they know where it's coming from, or by whom?"

"They don't know. They have a super powerful AI driven super-computer that reacts at the speed of light to threats. Over the past six hours, they've had their hands full protecting the system from a very sophisticated attacker that doesn't know enough to quit."

"They must be confident they have it under control. Despite my lack of knowledge of computers, as the owner of the system, I think they'd let me know if I was about to lose our biggest intel asset."

"Yeah, they seem to have it under control. But the attack is taking all of the machine's capacity, which has effectively shut down the search for our bad guys."

"It feels like we're losing the momentum. Omer and Abbas are in the hands of your interrogators. Have they given you anything useful?"

"No, not really. Omer had a slightly different agenda than Prince Turki. They threw in together because Omer wanted Turki's funding and they both had an axe to grind against Saudi, albeit for different reasons."

"I get that Turki wants payback for his Riyadh Ritz experience. What's Omer's grievance with the Kingdom?"

"Omer's a nationalist; he wants a return of the Ottoman Empire. He dreams of a second Turkish caliphate. Restoring the empire requires knocking down and then retaking pieces of the old empire. Saudi Arabia—especially Mecca and Medina—is an important part of the old empire's identity."

"That boy is delusional."

"He's bat shit crazy. All of the Grey Wolves are."

"What next?" I asked.

"The Director gave the order to take Prince Turki in. The cousins cooperated, and a team of MI-5 accompanied by our people went to his home in London to arrest him. They searched his estate and he was gone."

"Didn't you have him under surveillance?"

"We did, around the clock. We found a tunnel connecting to an adjacent building. He bolted and now we're trying to find him."

"Clearwater is great at those kinds of searches, but from what you've told me, they're not going to be any help this time, as they're too busy battling it out in cyberspace, fighting off the hacker hordes."

"We'll find him. He owns a lot of properties around the world, and it's going to take some time to check all of them."

"If he's dumb enough to hide in another place he owns. Although I'm sure they're all owned by untraceable shell companies. How's the situation in the region?"

"It's calming everywhere except Iran and Saudi. KSA is on the edge. The Saudi government may not be able to hold on; the situation is escalating into a full-blown civil war. Iran's fully mobilized, and is now cracking down hard on the protestors. The Mullahs looked to have stopped the revolution and will stay in charge."

"Do you think if we find Turki, he'll lead us to the source of the propaganda campaign, and that once we shut the social media network down the tensions will decline?"

"That's the plan."

"Sounds too easy. It's hard to believe people can be influenced so easily by media that you can incite a civil war with Twitter messages."

"The Spanish American War was purposely triggered by a media giant who planted a false report about the U.S.S. Maine. 'Remember the Maine, to hell with Spain' was yellow journalism at its peak. To this day, nobody knows why the Maine blew up in Havana harbor, but that didn't stop Hearst from fanning the flames until the US declared war on Spain. Never underestimate the power of the press. In the Middle East, they have ten times more faith in the accuracy of the internet and social media because the state-controlled television and print media have been feeding them propaganda for decades."

"I suppose it could be possible."

"It's definitely possible. We need to find Prince Turki; he's bound to know the source of the information campaign."

"He manages an empire. It can't be very easy for him to remain out of communication with his businesses for long."

"Believe me, we're working that angle. Having Clearwater distracted doesn't help."

"You're not the only one paying the price. I haven't seen Cheryl for days."

"What are you doing with yourself?"

"Lots of fishing. How much time do you have? If you want, we could leave now and get in a couple of hours."

"It's going to be dark soon."

"Haven't you ever heard of night fishing? It's a thing."

"Really?"

"Yeah."

"I can't; I have work. Don't you ever get bored with your life of leisure?"

"Never. What bores me is all this talk of cyber warfare. Nerds battling it out behind computer screens. The face of warfare has gone from Conan the Barbarian to Doctor Forrest. It's not a pretty sight."

"You're an anachronism."

"Yeah, and if that's not bad enough, I've lost the attention of my soulmate to the nerd warriors."

"That's what's really bothering you, isn't it?"

"Yeah, a little bit."

"Are you hungry, do you feel like grilling up some steaks?" Mike said while tapping the gas grill bolted in behind his chair.

We were downstairs in the Salon watching the first game of a Red Sox-Orioles double header. We had switched to wine; I found an Insignia 2012 Bordeaux from Napa, and I was showing Mike the reviews on my phone app when a text message came in from 99999999.

"From David Forrest. ALICE has been penetrated, disconnect all network devices from the internet and remove all power sources until further notification."

"Who's Alice?" I asked.

"ALICE is the name of Professor Forrest's artificial intelligence." As he was speaking, Mike looked at his phone. He must have received the same message.

"He was smart to keep that from me. I never would've let him play with the cool kids if I found out he was naming his computer."

"It stands for Artificial Learning Intelligent Computing Experiment; it's had that name since he first filed for grant money with the University of Edinburgh."

"That ends the ball game. I need to unplug everything on this boat connected to a network, and then we can drive to Clearwater and find out what's going on over there."

"What are you going to do about your iPhone?" Mike asked.

"I'm going to shut it off and put it in the Faraday box I keep downstairs. You should let me put yours in there too."

It took a full thirty minutes to unplug my personal computer, satellite dish, Apple TV, boat NAV system, and emergency locator beacon (EPIRB). I put the stuff with a battery that I couldn't remove, like the sat phones, iPhones and iPad, into the Faraday box I keep in the engine room. I've done enough tactical operations in stealth mode using the *Sam Houston* to know what systems connect to a network that could compromise my position. It wasn't the first time I'd been through the drill.

We drove to Clearwater in Mike's rental; he said the opposition could hack into the OnStar on my Suburban, but they were less likely to know about his rental.

"This scenario has a 2001 Space Odyssey quality to it," I said.

"HAL, is that you?" Mike replied.

When we arrived at Clearwater, we couldn't get into the building. The security system had been disabled and the card reader and biometric reader were not operating. I banged on the heavy steel door for fifteen minutes before Cheryl finally opened it. She was soaked with sweat, her hair was in a ponytail and all she was wearing were running shorts and a t-shirt. The hangar was sweltering hot.

"What's going on?" I asked.

"I'm disconnecting all of your equipment. The plane, the helicopters, the drones, the communications systems, the navigation aids. It's too much; I could use a hand."

"I'm on it. How far did you get?" I said.

"Both of the unmanned helicopters are disabled. I started with the most dangerous first. Everything else still needs to be disconnected."

"Sachse, McDonald, Migos, and Jankowski showed up within the next hour. It took another three hours to get everything unplugged. The air conditioning returned as we were finishing up."

Sitting around the conference room table there were eight of us drinking sodas. We were all dirty and sweaty. David Forrest looked the worst. He's older and heavier than the rest of the team to begin with, and the overwork and lack of sleep were taking a heavy toll. This was the first time I'd ever seen him without a sports jacket. He looked completely distraught and broken.

"What just happened?" I asked.

"ALICE was penetrated. It was a complete breach. Before they overtook everything, ALICE sent a dying-breath message to everyone connected, or who have been connected to the Clearwater network, to protect themselves from further infiltration."

"The bad guys got into your computer system. What did they take?" I asked.

"Everything. A complete data theft. Not only that, they almost succeeded in taking control of ALICE. They were the ones who were shutting off lights, locking doors and taking control of the hangar."

"Is that it? Is everything OK now?"

"No, far from it. The people who launched the attack were able to defeat one of the most advanced AI systems in the world. ALICE is powered by a CRAY supercomputer; very few people in the world own that much computing power, and even fewer have the programming skills to do what was done tonight. These people now know everything ALICE knew about you and about Clearwater."

"This is a total security breach," Mike said.

"Yes, and we've been networked to CIA, NSA, NRO, FBI, DOD & JSOC networks with ALICE. Everything is compromised. They know who Clearwater is, and they know who every one of you are. I think you should expect them to go after your personal life, your financials and every other aspect of your life that can be harmed through a computer. These people mean serious business."

"The government agencies have their own firewalls. I'm sure they haven't been breached," Mike said.

"Not yet they haven't, and whoever did this, probably doesn't want to take on the US Government. It's already toppling several in the Middle East, and it just killed ALICE," David said with enough emotion to make one believe he had just lost his wife.

"Jankowski's going to have his Tinder account hacked. That's going to create serious havoc at the local high school," said Migos.

"Let's stay focused. Before ALICE caught a bullet on the digital battlefield, did we learn anything about where this attack was coming from?" I asked.

"No, but we did learn some things that may help in narrowing it down," David Forrest said.

"OK, narrow it down for us."

"The attacker has greater capabilities than we do, which means they have faster computational speed which requires a very well-funded organization with top programmers. They most likely were using some form of artificial intelligence," David said.

"How many organizations in the world fit that profile, and where are they?"

"There are roughly four hundred and fifty supercomputers in service around the world. There are eleven manufacturers. Almost all of the manufacturers are in the US, except for three in Japan, and one in China. NUDT in China has built the world's most powerful computer and the Chinese have the worst reputation for this sort of thing."

"Do you think this attack came from China?" I asked.

"Doubtful. We were able to trace the path of some of the code used against us, and I believe the origin is in the Middle East or North Africa."

"What you're telling us is that we need to locate every super computer in the world, all four hundred and fifty or whatever the real number is. And if we can find a system that's located in the Middle East or North Africa, we'll have found our attacker," I said.

"It will narrow down the suspects," David answered.

"We keep track of that information. I'll reach back to Langley and get you answers ASAP."

"What are we going to do now about communications?" asked Migos.

"I am going to restore ALICE from backup and keep her offline until I know I can protect against another penetration. Understand that what just happened is the exploitation. They took hundreds of terabytes of information. What they do with that information will be the actual attack. We don't know what that attack will be, or when it will happen," David said.

"Don't you think the purpose of the penetration was to get you offline because you were searching for the source of the information campaign against the Saudis?" Mike asked.

"Sure, it's possible they'll stop now that ALICE is offline. But, I don't think we should assume that will be the case," David said.

"That doesn't answer my question; how do we communicate?" Migos asked.

"Burner cellphones. Assume an alias ID until this is over," I replied.

"What's the impact on Trident?" Cheryl asked Dave.

"Clearwater does the intel workup for every Trident mission, even the routine cargo deliveries. They took a lot of information on Trident they can use. What they didn't get is any of the logistics and financial data that flows between Trident and the US Government agencies."

"That's good news, so they probably didn't drain the Trident bank accounts yet," I said.

"These guys are good enough to do that. You should add extra protections to everything you do online," he said.

It was getting late, and I tried to get Cheryl to return back to the boat with me, but she refused. I settled for sharing her twin bed in her office bedroom. She was exhausted and fell asleep as soon as her head hit the pillow. Words cannot describe my disappointment.

I woke up the next morning alone. I put on a fresh pair of jeans and a black t-shirt that said Glacier Rafting and headed out to find coffee. In the kitchen area of the Trident side of the hangar, I found a fresh pot of coffee and a box of donuts. Holding out the donuts was Migos. He seemed particularly pleased with himself.

"What's with the grin? Don't you know we're experiencing cyber Armageddon here?"

"I know boss, it's serious, but watching you wander around aimlessly is just funny as hell."

"I'm not wandering aimlessly. I came to the kitchen focused like a laser on coffee and donuts."

"Admit it; you have no idea what to do in this situation."

"Of course, I do. I'm going to find these hacker geeks and then I'm going to strangle them. But first, I'm going to eat this jelly donut."

"Boss, what we're seeing here is the future and I don't think you have a place in it."

"In the immortal words of Yogi Berra, the future isn't what it used to be."

"What does that mean?"

"Computer hackers will never replace soldiers. If the nerds figure out how to disable modern weapons, that just means future wars will be fought the old-fashioned way, with swords and spears."

"You think so?"

"Yeah, I do. Right now, there's a computer whiz somewhere out there, filled with self-confidence and absolutely thrilled with himself for shutting down our network. He's probably more stoked about re-wiring the social media platforms. But when guys like that break the modern technology, guys like us counter old school. Everybody has a weakness. To quote the great philosopher Yogi, 'even Napoleon had his Watergate.'"

"Don't underestimate the computer whiz."

"I won't, but he shouldn't underestimate us, just because his computer beat up our computer."

A low-pitched wail was heard over the hum of the hangar air conditioning system.

"What was that?" Migos asked.

"I don't know; it sounded like one of the Ents in Lord of the Rings," I said, before taking a bite out of my donut. Then we heard it again.

"It's coming from the Clearwater office. Let's check it out."

I took a 9mm P226 from the weapons locker on my way to the Clearwater wing. We went through reception into the computer room. Cheryl was standing over Doctor Forrest who was seated behind a computer console. Dave's hands were covering his face and he was making deep guttural sounds that can only be described as what absolute anguish sounds like.

"What's wrong?" I asked.

"GSS in Scotland has been compromised; that's the first thing we learned this morning. We have contagion. When David tried to turn ALICE on this morning, he was locked out of the system. He's received a ransom message," Cheryl said.

"The computer's being held hostage?" I said.

"Yes," Cheryl said.

"Can I see the message?"

"It's still on the screen."

"Migos, can you sedate Doctor Forrest? The poor guy hasn't slept in days, and he's useless in his current state." Migos grabbed the semi-catatonic David from his chair and led him away from the computer console. Like most special operations units, the guys on our team had a mini-pharmacy at their disposal. I was sure Migos would find a way to guarantee Doctor Forrest a good twelve hours of rest.

I looked at the screen to see the message.

"Transfer ten million dollars to the swift code and account number below and you will receive the password to access your computer," it said.

"What does this mean?" I asked.

"It means they inserted a Trojan horse in the backup. Dave stayed up all night scrubbing and cleaning the drives, then when he restored the system from the backup, he brought in the ransomware."

"That's just great."

"Are you going to pay?"

"No, I don't think these guys care about the money. If I tried to transfer money to them, they'd probably hijack my bank account or do some other mischief. I'd rather just ask them for the password face-to-face."

"We need to find them."

"Mike's people are working on it. You should focus on the same; do some old-fashioned intelligence work, pre-ALICE. David will be good after some rest, and then he can help out," I said.

"Do you think so?"

"I've been so tired before that I've had hallucinations. Migos will put him down, and when he wakes up, he'll be good to go."

"He lost ALICE 2 here with Clearwater, and now he's lost ALICE 1 with GSS in Edinburgh. The man is devastated; it's his life's work."

"You should notify GSS of what could happen if they try to restore from backup," I said.

"Good idea, the backup of ALICE 1 is all he has left," she said.

CHAPTER 22

Tangier, Morocco

Prince Turki was on a PlayStation 4 located in his palace in Tangiers. He forbade his servants and his mistress from entering the entertainment room during his daily noon gaming ritual. He scrolled through the "God of War" menu, and made his way into the chat room. He found a private message from XOES: "I have vanquished Aphrodite; she's off the board," the message read. Aphrodite is the Greek goddess who lived in Cyprus, and the message meant that his man had neutralized the source of the intrusions that had been coming from Cyprus over the past week. Prince Turki typed: "Congratulations on your victory. How goes the campaign to the East?" he messaged under the username NEJD.

"Fighting escalates daily. Casualties yesterday reached seventeen hundred dead, many times that wounded. Military and police salaries were not paid this month due to a computer glitch (he he), but social media reports it's because several key leaders have fled the country with the funds. Defections among security forces are growing. Estimated time to victory is projected to be between four to six weeks." XOES.

The news brought a smile to Prince Turki's face. He erased the messages and shut the system off. Except for the daily update on the computer game chat-board with a man he liked to think of as his general in the field, he used no other media devices. He banned all cell phones and computers from the house. His favorite Moroccan mistress was particularly upset about being denied her iPhone, but he was able to overcome her protests about Facebook withdrawal with the promise of a new car. He needed to lie low for only another six weeks. Final victory was so close he could taste it.

CHAPTER 23

Paphos, Cyprus

Communications were restored, and Clearwater returned to operations without its feature asset, ALICE, a name I had never heard until the crisis. Cheryl soldiered on without the aid of supercomputer-powered artificial intelligence. David returned to Scotland to nurse his precious ALICE 1 back to health. ALICE 2 remained a hostage to the nefarious computer hackers. Cheryl was working more reasonable hours and coming home to the boat at night. The Trident cargo deliveries and resultant revenue resumed. Everything was not completely back to normal, but two weeks after the cyber-attack, a sense of normalcy and equilibrium had been achieved.

I was in the galley fixing a chicken stir fry when Cheryl walked in. I turned when she opened the triple sliding doors leading into the salon. She looked magnificent; she always does. She's drop dead gorgeous and knows it. She's fashion model thin and, at 5'7", she's exceptionally tall for a Chinese woman. She came up behind me and wrapped her arms around my waist. I put down the spatula, turned and gave her a hug. She has a tiny waist and a really nice body; I like holding her a lot.

"How was your day?" I asked.

"Good, we're making progress."

"That's nice."

"We've had to create an ad hoc team between the Agency and Clearwater. It's too early to say for certain, but I think we're close to a breakthrough."

"Anything I can do?" I asked.

"No, this isn't your thing. Do I have time to change?"

"Yeah, if you hurry."

I finished up and set the table. Cheryl joined me on the bench seat at the galley table as I was serving.

"What no wine, no beer?" she said.

"It goes right to my hips," I said. "I have sparkling water with lemon and, by the way, thanks for asking about my day."

"What do you mean?" she said.

"I cook, I clean, I work so hard. Today I ran, I lifted, I went to the pistol range, I detailed the engine room and serviced the tender. You didn't ask, you didn't even notice what I'm wearing, that I put on my brand new Under Armour t-shirt tonight that accentuates my biceps and shrinks my waist to get your attention."

"Are you feeling underappreciated, darling?"

"Yes, and it wouldn't hurt if you took me out once in a while. I have feelings, you know."

Cheryl started to giggle and then transitioned to a full out laugh. It was contagious, and I did the same.

"Look at us," she said with a smile.

"Total role reversal. The world is upside down, dogs sleeping with cats, the works."

A breakthrough arrived, but it didn't come from Clearwater. It arrived the old-fashioned way, from the CIA station in Egypt. It was almost entirely by accident. A member of the Egyptian MOI on the CIA payroll supplied information on a content-farming operation in Cairo to his handler. MOI was monitoring a subject who worked at the facility.

The facility had all of the appearances of a legitimate operation. It was a registered company. Alexandria Marketing Services was a call center that provided contract support to a number of major retail brand-name electronics manufacturers in the Middle East. AMS had over three hundred service representatives working on each of its three shifts. The company owned an eight-story building in the Al-Zaytoun area of Cairo near the airport. Like most of Cairo, Al-Zaytoun is a heavily congested urban area. The AMS building was nondescript and nothing about the operations stood out. If the MOI had not been tailing a political activist who also happened to work at AMS, it likely never would've been identified as a content farm. The MOI was lucky when they found it, and the CIA was lucky when they found out about it from MOI. The Egyptian authorities are not all that friendly to the USA these days, and the Egyptian government doubtlessly has no objections to the content-farming operation. Had one of the MOI investigators not been on the CIA payroll, it's unlikely the US ever would've known of its existence.

I flew to Dubai with Cheryl to meet Mike. He was on a layover, but couldn't share any of the details. Le Meridien in Dubai is an old, sprawling, three floor airport hotel. Cheryl and I flew Emirates and then took a taxi from Terminal 3 to the hotel, which was less than a mile away. We met Mike in his room.

"Cheryl, you look fantastic!" Mike said after giving Cheryl a hug.

"Thank you, Michael. It's nice to no longer be reminded of our experience in Istanbul every time I look in the mirror."

"Well, you're as beautiful as ever."

"Did I tell you I'm cutting down on the carbs and I've dropped an inch in my waistline?" I mentioned.

"Hey Pat, yeah that's good to know," Mike said taking Cheryl by the arm and leading her to the couch in the sitting area.

I followed and sat next to Cheryl on the couch, across the coffee table from Mike who was seated on a lounge chair.

"Based on the information provided by Clearwater before the cyberattack crashed your system and what we've discovered, this is how we think the information war is being waged.

"There's at least one content farm where social media messages, YouTube videos, and images are being created by fake users and sent out to the Twittersphere to undermine the Saudi Government.

"In addition to the synthetic messaging, there are also organic messages being created from actual Saudi users that are harmful to the Saudi Government.

"On the major platforms—Facebook, Twitter, Instagram, WhatsApp— the anti-government messages are reaching subscribers who are not followers, friends and addressees. The anti-government messages are reaching an audience many multiples beyond the normal ranges of the social media services. Pro-government messages are having the opposite experience.

"The barriers Saudi has in place to shut down and limit access to the internet are not working. Widespread use of VPNs by the people is one reason. A bigger reason is hacks into the Saudi communication companies that are shutting down the gateways that filter communications. This has thwarted the Saudi Government's ability to counter the threat.

"Believe it or not, we have a good working relationship with the heads of the major social media companies. We're all in the information business. We're convinced they're not complicit, but we believe their platforms have been compromised in some way, so as to make the anti-government messages more effective.

"By more effective, I mean geometric multiples more effective. The same message sent out to an audience with the same number of followers will actually reach a hugely different number of subscribers, 1000 to 1 in some instances where it has been tracked. A pro-government message will reach a thousand people, while an anti-government message is reaching a million, and that's when both senders have the same number of contacts or followers in their network."

"Can't you request the social media companies stop it?" Cheryl asked.

"We have, but it's not that easy, because it shouldn't happen, and they don't know how it's happening."

"And you believe them?" Cheryl said.

"We do. There's no motive or reason why all four of these publicly traded companies would incite a revolution," Mike said.

"But they are."

"Each of them is diving into the inner workings of their code to figure out how their systems are being co-opted; they'll get it figured out eventually. In the meantime, we need to disable the content-farming operations," he said.

"This must be why I was invited to this meeting," I said

"Exactly, we have a target package of AMS managers we want you to capture. We want to interrogate them for any clues connecting the content farm to Silicon Valley, and we want the site permanently disabled."

"Do you have a plan?"

"It's a work in progress. A modified CHAMP device is being shipped to your headquarters in Paphos. The fastest and easiest way to permanently take out hundreds, possibly thousands of computers, servers, tablets, phones and electronic devices at the AMS building is with an EMP weapon."

"CHAMP is an EMP weapon?"

"It stands for Counter-electronics High Power Microwave Advanced Missile Project. It's designed to go on a cruise missile, but we're sending you a system that's fitted onto the bed of a full-sized pickup truck. It has enough power to fry every electronic device inside the AMS building."

"You want us to drive an EMP device to the AMS building and explode it?"

"Yes, but it doesn't explode; it pulses a directed beam of microwave energy. The device is safe for humans, and only kills electronics. This one has been modified. The EMP will create an ultra-high frequency field with a range of up to 3.5 kilometers, and has a hundred gigawatts of power, which is a nuclear level EMP burst. I've been assured it will destroy every electronic in the AMS building and maybe even one or two of the buildings nearby."

"OK, so we land in Cairo. Drive to AMS. Kidnap the three guys on this target list and nuke the electronics."

"Yes."

"How do we get an EMP device through customs at the Cairo Airport?"

"The system we deliver will be inside the housing of a 30KW generator. The people at customs won't be able to tell the difference. Pay the duties and fees on the fake generator and drive it away."

"What do we do with it when we're done? Is it a one-time use?"

"It's reusable. You'll make two shots against the target to be sure and when you're done, you need to demolish it and make sure it can't be copied by our opposition. There's only enough power in the battery for two shots."

"OK, we can figure out the rest with what you gave us," I said.

"What are the backgrounds of the three guys on the target list?"

"Dr. Hany Al-Sahkowi and Dr. Ahmed Zahran are Muslim Brotherhood. Both are faculty members at Cairo University in addition to being Senior VPs at AMS."

"What do they teach?"

"Sahkowi teaches sociology. Zahran teaches political science."

"Who's the third guy?"

"The CEO, Osama Attiyais, is a Qatari citizen. He spends most of his time in Doha, and only visits the facility for a few days each month. The daily operations are managed by Sahkowi and Zahran. We think Attiyais is the money man."

"He probably won't be at the facility when we attack; we'll have to grab him later."

CHAPTER 24

Cairo, Egypt.

I drove my rented Citroen C5 past the AMS building for the second time. We had two days to wait for the pickup truck carrying the fake generator to clear customs, and I was using the time to conduct reconnaissance. It was the afternoon rush hour, and I was creeping along in front of the AMS building while the sound of car horns filled the air. I was scanning for available parking in front of the building when a van abruptly cut in front of me. I jammed on the brakes, narrowly missing the rear bumper of the van by inches. Cairo traffic and the bizarre behavior of the local drivers were going to make the timing of this operation challenging.

I returned to the Hilton, made a quick change, and located the gym. After lifting, I did another change and headed to the pool for a swim workout. My latest workout kick is fifty-meter sprints. After fifteen or twenty, I'm exhausted; it's a great combination strength and cardio workout. The Hilton has three pools—a lap pool, a kiddy pool, and a big pool for the loungers. I try to limit the break between sprints to thirty seconds, but by the last one, I took over a minute. I had trouble hoisting myself up the ladder to get out of the pool. On my way back to my room, I found the other four guys occupying loungers next to the pool. There was some kind of conference going on at the hotel and whatever business the attendees were involved in, it required some of the prettiest girls in North Africa. If I had to guess, I'd say cosmetics, fashion, or pharmaceutical sales.

We were supposed to meet later in my room for the final go, no-go briefing, but I decided to get it over with.

"Let's talk," I said as I stepped out of my flip flops and jumped into the pool. The other guys followed me into the shallow end. I looked around and made sure it wasn't possible for anyone to listen in.

"Where's the truck?" I asked McDonald.

"It's in the eastern parking lot. Not too far from the lobby."

"Did you check it out."

"It passed the diagnostic routines I was given."

"What time did Sahkowi and Zahron make it into work this morning?" I asked Migos.

"Zahron showed up at 8:45 and Sahkowi at 11:10," he said.

"Did you put the trackers on their cars?" I asked.

"They both have drivers who drop them off, because it's impossible to get a parking spot in that area. We had to follow them. Burnia tagged Zahron's car after his driver stopped at a coffee house. Jankowski caught Sahkowi's when his driver stopped for afternoon prayer," Migos said.

"We're a go for tomorrow. We'll execute on order, when both Shriners are at work." We nicknamed the two targets as Shriner 1 and Shriner 2 after Zahron was seen wearing a red fez hat like the one sported by the Shriners.

"We're off tonight, boss," Migos said returning the attention of two young ladies sitting on the stairs leading into the shallow in. They were both looking our way.

"Stay focused Romeo, we're on an operation."

"If I don't go and say hello, that would be a big red star-cluster telling the world that we're on an operation. You don't want me to blow our cover, do you?"

"No, of course not. Don't get stupid."

"Burnia, I need a wing-man and it's time you began your education at the feet of the master. Come Padawan, let's go." The two broke off from our group. It wasn't hard to figure out what the two ladies were staring at; Burnia, Jankowski and Migos are physical specimens. Combined, the three don't have a bodyfat content adding up to over twenty percent. I left to shower and coordinate our exit from Egypt with the aircrew who were staying at the neighboring Sheraton.

The next day, I was seated in the passenger side of the pickup truck that was carrying the CHAMP. McDonald was beside me at the wheel. We were both looking at a tablet that was propped up on the center console of the dash. We were following a circular red icon as it traversed across a map of the city. I touched the covert transmit button on my ring.

"Shriner 2 approaching objective; ETA five miles."

"Romeo, are you in position?" I decided to call Migos 'Romeo' for this operation. He was in a stolen van with Burnia and Jankowski, along with McDonald and my backup electronics.

"Romeo is set, as is Padawan and the Monk. Just in case you're wondering, our boy grew up last night. Padawan is no longer an innocent. I say again 'the eagle has landed,'" I heard over the Bluetooth earbud in my right ear.

"Clear the net," I said.

I was wearing running shoes, blue jeans, and a loose, short-sleeve button down. I had a Walther 9mm tucked into a concealed holster that was irritating my back. We waited until the icon stopped in front of the AMS building before getting on the road. I wanted both Shriners in the executive office suite on the eighth floor where I could find them.

It took almost ten minutes to reach the AMS headquarters, as we hit every light and the traffic was as bad as expected. All of the parking spots on both sides of the road in front of the building were occupied. McDonald double-parked our white Ford F150 as close to the front entranceway as he could get. We both got out of the truck. The traffic began to back up and horns began to blare. McDonald dropped the tailgate, stepped into the bed, and began to work at the operator's console. I opened the hood to signal to the angry car drivers that we had a maintenance problem. It didn't seem to matter to at least five of the backed-up drivers who were leaning on their horns without stop.

"Firing," I heard McDonald's voice say inside my earbud. The CHAMP started making a loud whine like a jet engine spooling up and then it stopped. When it did, the horns from the angry drivers stopped with it. Peace at last. I tossed my phone, earbud, and PTT ring into the back of the cab and walked around to the tailgate. I checked the AMS building and I couldn't see any lights, but it was daylight and the building doesn't have a lot of windows, so I wasn't completely sure the first pulse did the trick. The CHAMP spooled up again and just the same as the first time, the whining suddenly stopped. McDonald opened a five-gallon jerry can of gas and began dumping it on top of the CHAMP and on top of the cab of the vehicle. He jumped off and I handed him two thermite grenades. He tossed both of his on top of the CHAMP. I threw one in the cab and another on top of the engine. Our vehicle went up in flames.

We waited on the sidewalk with the rest of the crowd that was distracted by the burning pickup truck. Most in the crowd divided their time between trying to make their phones work and watching the truck melt. Migos, Burnia, and Jankowski were running up the sidewalk toward us. Jankowski handed a bag to McDonald; in it was his replacement comm set.

"The van is parked two hundred yards back, the corner of Horeya and Gabal. Here are the keys; it's a black Mercedes van." Migos handed me a bag, and I put my new comm set into operation. I tucked the flashlight into my pants pocket. It had been five minutes since the EMP fired and nobody had left the building yet. The four of us headed toward the entryway.

When we entered the building, we were stopped in the lobby by a security guard. He was holding a pistol in his right hand. The entry had a metal detector and two turnstiles that required key cards to pass. Behind the turnstiles was a bank of four elevators and a stairwell entrance. A second security guard was stationed by an X-ray machine. At the sight of the drawn pistol, I held my hands up. The guard appeared confused. He had the microphone connected to his hand-held radio in his other hand, and he appeared to be trying to get directions on what to do from his supervisor, but he had no way of knowing a CHAMP EMP weapon had fried his radio. From behind me, Burnia shot the security guard through the forehead. The second guard who was still seated behind the X-ray machine was taken out by Jankowski. I hopped the turnstile and went for the stairwell.

The four of us raced up eight flights of stairs with our flashlights in front of us to guide our steps. The stairwell was pitch black, and the lack of air conditioning was beginning to heat things up. We didn't pass anyone on the stairs. When we reached the eighth floor, I opened the door and let Alpha Team through. Burnia and Jankowski burst through. They weren't the slightest bit winded; I hate youth. Migos and I followed. Unlike the other floors, the eighth had a lot of windows.

Burnia and Jankowski were standing in the reception area with pistols drawn. The receptionist was lying flat on the ground. The poor woman was in a lot of distress; she was morbidly obese, and she had her hands and feet flex cuffed and a cloth gag wrapped tightly around her mouth. I led Migos past Bravo Team into the corridor leading to the offices. We entered the first office; it was empty.

Burnia and Jankowski hopped past us and entered the second office.

"Jackpot, Shriner 2," I heard over the comm set.

I walked into the next office. Shriner 1 was sitting behind his desk. Another employee was sitting on the opposite side of his desk. I walked up to him and leveled my pistol at his face.

"Doctor Zahron, you can either come with me, or you can die where you stand." He held up his hands and began to walk toward the door. The second man stood to protest, and Migos, using his flashlight like a baton, whipped him unconscious with a single forehand stroke.

The trip down the stairs was a much slower affair than the run up. A trickle of people from the other floors had begun to attempt to navigate the pitch-black stairwell. The EMP pulse made sure there were no working flashlights in the building. We passed through the turnstiles and entered the street. The truck was still burning. It was a black, smoking fire now.

Migos and I guided Zahron around the building and down a side street. Jankowski and McDonald were doing the same with Sakhowi.

"Driver, are you set?" I said into my comms.

"Affirmative," McDonald replied.

We found McDonald and the van and tossed the two Shriners into the back.

We dumped the stolen van and transferred our cargo to our rented van. We dropped two heavy pelican boxes off to our CIA Liaison at the US Embassy. Inside the boxes were two heavily sedated Egyptians with supplemental oxygen tanks. The boxes marked with a diplomatic exemption were escorted by embassy personnel through customs and loaded onto the C130 less than two hours later. We dropped the cargo at Bagram Air Force Base in Afghanistan and handed the Shriners over to a team of waiting CIA interrogators.

CHAPTER 25

Bainbridge, Washington

Evan Moskowitz leaned forward from the couch and with a rolled up hundred-dollar bill snorted a line of white powder into his nose. He looked up at the skylight fifty feet above him as he felt the blood rush to his head and then he bent forward again and licked the remnants of the cocaine powder from the navel of a young girl.

He picked up his drink and sat back on the couch. The naked, blonde B-list actress whose teeny bopper vampire romances he'd never seen, rolled onto her stomach and with a razor blade prepared a line of coke for herself on the smooth glass surface of the coffee table. Pounding electronic dance music filled the room. Through his drug-induced haze, he looked out through the huge glass windows that made up the east wall of the great room. It was dawn, and the first rays of sunlight were filtering through the lush greenery of the virgin coniferous forest outside. Through the gaps in the giant tree trunks, he could see the cold, dark waters of the Puget Sound. He felt arms gently wrap around his neck. He reached back and pulled Ziggy, his popstar girlfriend, over the couch and onto his lap. The twenty-two-year old music sensation from Barbados had two songs in the top ten of the charts. She was glassy eyed, smiling and playful. The two had shared a hit of acid hours earlier, and Ziggy was just now coming down for a soft landing.

Evan had been celebrating all week. In his last conference call with his blood-sucking investors, he'd announced that his electric car company had stopped hemorrhaging cash. For the first time in the company's history, he'd achieved a positive cash flow and the company was only months away from realizing its first profitable quarter. Skyrocketing gas prices caused by the crisis in the Middle East had rescued his sales and drowned out the bad press from the exploding battery fiasco that had been irritating him all year. Production problems had been resolved and five thousand cars a month were now rolling off the assembly line. The long position he'd taken in the futures market produced the final two billion dollars he needed to avert defaulting on the upcoming rollover on part of his company's gargantuan sixty-two billion dollars of debt. Life was going his way; he'd escaped disaster yet again. The founder, original programmer, and forced-out CEO of the largest internet search engine company on the planet owed his salvation to his friend and business associate, Prince Turki.

He couldn't resist spiting his detractors, especially his most hated enemies, the hedge fund managers who had been so outspoken in their criticism of his management decisions. Especially galling was the public shorting of his stock as they foretold his imminent demise. At the height of his acid trip, he'd taken a picture of the lithe B-lister dressed only in a pair of his oversize, custom-made boxers. The blonde sex symbol had to hold the shorts up by the waist to keep them on. He sent a waist-down shot of the girl wearing his underwear with the caption "Volta Stock Surges, Eat my Shorts" out on Twitter to all of his followers. The recent 27% surge in his stock price, combined with this apparently witty double entendre Twitter message, had gone viral and set the fawning tech media aflame. He was once again being hailed as a genius maverick visionary forging America's path into the new economy. It felt great to be back on top.

CHAPTER 26

Tangiers, Morocco

Prince Turki typed into the private messaging on his God of War game: "Cairo has fallen," he wrote.

Seconds later a response came from the username XOES: "How?"

"Both professors were taken. All of the hardware has been destroyed."

"Destroyed? In what way?"

"I don't know. All of the electronics were fried, the data destroyed. Two security guards were killed, Zahron and Sahkowi captured. This is a huge setback."

"We can still reach the goal. This will only slow the inevitable; it won't prevent it."

"Zahron and Sahkowi will talk."

"Do they know about me?"

"No, but they know there is help from the platforms and that could lead an investigation your way."

"Who's doing the investigating?"

"The CIA and a contractor."

"How do you know?"

"Egyptian Intelligence is piecing together the attack. A CIA contracting company, Trident, landed a Hercules transport in Cairo three days before the attack. They departed hours after the attack, but not before receiving a diplomatic shipment that bypassed customs. The Egyptians believe Zahron and Sahkowi were in that diplomatic shipment."

"Has the Egyptian government filed a protest?"

"No, the Egyptian government doesn't want to pick a fight with the US Government. They were harboring an organization that was actively destabilizing Saudi Arabia, and that's not exactly something they want to advertise."

"Trident? is that the same group you asked me to take offline?"

"That was Clearwater, a company owned by Trident."

"What do you want me to do?"

"The cyber-attack didn't work. We can't have any more interference from Trident. We need to do something that is more permanent. More physical."

"Let me look into it. I'll get back to you."

Evan Moskowitz closed the game program. He felt terrible, his head was pounding, and his hands had a mild tremor. He contacted his helicopter service and dressed for a trip to his headquarters in Seattle. He owned the company that stored the servers used by the FBI and other government agencies. He was also a leader in the private space industry. He had built backdoors into the software of his old search engine company. He had all the private sector and government resources he needed at his disposal; this wouldn't be hard. Once in his office, he would access the mainframe and unlock the Clearwater program he was holding ransom. He would find out everything he could about this group that was antagonizing his friend Prince Turki and then put an end to it.

CHAPTER 27

Paphos, Cyprus

I woke early. I could hear the waves gently lapping against the hull of the *Sam Houston*. I used the remote, and the large screen TV across from the bed came to life. I scrolled through the Apple TV menu and found MLB.TV It was a little after 4:00 a.m. in Cyprus, but it was 9:00-something in the evening at Boston's Fenway Park. It was the seventh inning and the Red Sox were losing 1-0 to Tampa.

I went upstairs and returned with a cup of coffee. I lay at the edge of the bed, leaving Cheryl undisturbed in the center. She was asleep, but like a heat-seeking missile she crept across the bed until she was next to me, and eventually she rolled over and blanketed me. She made it impossible to sip my coffee, so I gave up on it. I put my arms around her and held on as the Sox went hitless for the final three innings. When the game ended, I decided somebody from Boston needed to score this day, and so I woke her with a gentle persistent touch under the covers.

We drove to the hangar together. Cheryl went into the Clearwater wing. I stayed in the open hangar and talked with the guys. Migos was operating a remote-controlled forklift, moving air pallets from the hangar floor into the cargo hold of the C130. The five aluminum pallets still in the hangar were covered with yellow nylon-mesh webbing. Each pallet was stacked shoulder high with 82mm mortar rounds. Later in the morning, the Hercules was going to deliver the load to the Peshmerga in Northern Syria.

The C130 was parked outside the hangar with its tailgate open and ramp down facing the hangar. Inside the cargo plane, I could see Bill Sachse tying down the first pallet. Off to the side of the open bay area of the hangar was the gym. Burnia and Jankowski were inside the open-air enclave. Jankowski was swinging a kettle bell. Burnia was alternating between the chin up bar and snapping two heavy ropes up and down. I'll never understand this CrossFit stuff. Mitch Dornan and Bryan Patton, the two pilots from the flight crew, were at a table in the room next to the gym, both seated in the open kitchen area drinking coffee.

I was near the ramp of the C130 when I first noticed it. A refueler truck was rolling toward our location. This was not an uncommon sight and it seemed likely the Hercules needed to be fueled before takeoff. The vehicle moved slowly as it chugged toward the plane. Instead of stopping, it narrowly missed the wing tip of the airplane and kept moving forward toward the hangar opening. The truck continued into the hangar. I watched it helplessly. When the truck reached the center of the hangar area, it exploded. I was standing next to the C130 back ramp and the blast knocked me backwards onto my ass. I lay back and flattened my body on the tarmac as a wave of searing heat swept over me. Secondary explosions from the mortar rounds inside the hangar began to cook off.

I was sitting on the ground looking into the hangar when I heard the tail ramp of the C130 begin to rise and the engines come to life. A quick-thinking Sachse gunned the propellers and taxied the aircraft away from the conflagration. The hangar entry was a curtain of smoke, and every few seconds I could hear another mortar round explode. I saw movement, and then a body emerged from the smoke. It was Migos. He collapsed when he reached the sunlight. I ran to him and dragged him to safety out on the tarmac.

The airport firetrucks and EMS arrived within ten minutes. Migos was standing unsteadily next to an ambulance. The firefighters waited until the mortar rounds stopped cooking off before turning on the foaming hoses. The metal roof of the hangar was partially collapsed, with smoke billowing out the top. I tried to go into the hangar, but a firefighter stopped me. I ran to the C130 Sachse had parked a thousand yards distant and came back with a HALO mask. I put the mask on my face, turned on the small bottle of compressed air and made my way toward the hangar. The same firefighter stood in front of me and pointed for me to go back. I swept him aside with a brush of my arm and headed into the smoke.

Visibility was only a few feet in the main hangar. I had a good air supply and the mask kept the smoke from my eyes. From memory, I paced the route and direction to the Clearwater office. The entry door was blown off; I entered the corridor. The fabric-covered hallway walls were burning and flames ran up the sides of the walls. I passed the reception area and headed to Cheryl's office. Visibility was only a few feet. When I didn't see her, I looked for the entry into her sleeping area. The door was still intact, which was a good sign. The door, as it opened, swept aside a wet towel that must have been placed by her to prevent smoke from entering under the door. The smoke in the bedroom was not as bad as outside. I looked around and still couldn't find Cheryl. I went into the bathroom and found her sitting in the glass shower with her arms around her knees. A pall of smoke hung above her in the air.

I removed my mask.

"Are you all right?"

"Yes, what happened?"

"Explosion. The hangar is on fire; we need to leave"

"OK."

"Outside this room, the smoke is very bad. I'm going to give you my mask. You lead the way out. I'll hold on to you while I hold my breath."

"OK."

I put the HALO mask onto Cheryl's face. It's a full-faced mask and I could see her expression brighten as she drank up the clean air. I took a towel from the bathroom and put it over my mouth.

"Let's go!"

When we opened the door into her office, the smoke was heavy but manageable. When we entered the reception area it became impossible for me to either see or breathe. I held onto Cheryl's shoulder as she led our way out. By the time we made it to the hangar, my lungs were screaming for oxygen. I kept my right hand on her shoulder and followed her every step. Eventually, through eyes streaming with tears, I could see a lightness from the hangar opening.

I almost made it; my head felt like it was about to explode, my lungs were screaming for air and, out of desperation, I took a breath. I dropped to my knees, hacking and filling my lungs full of black smoke, and then I blacked out. We were close enough to the exterior that two firefighters in oxygen gear saw what was happening, rushed into the hangar, and dragged me to safety.

I regained consciousness in an ambulance wearing an oxygen mask. Cheryl was next to me.

"Where's everybody else?" I asked in a raspy voice.

"Migos, Sachse, and McDonald are outside," she said.

"McDonald?"

"He just got here."

"Burnia, Jankowski, Dornan, and Patton?"

"They didn't make it out," she said, without any hint of expression.

I fell back onto the ambulance stretcher and let that news sink in.

CHAPTER 28

Abu Dhabi, UAE

We moved the cargo operations to our alternate site at Darfur Air Force base, where Trident maintained a hangar. Cheryl was in Scotland, working with Doctor Forrest at the GSS office near the University of Edinburgh. ALICE 1 was back online. ALICE 2 was no longer a hostage; it had been completely destroyed in the fire and with its backup destroyed weeks earlier, its very existence had been erased. Cray had already shipped a replacement to Edinburgh and Doctor Forrest was working marathon hours recreating his lost love.

It was going to take much longer to rebuild the hangar in Paphos. In addition to the tragic loss of our personnel, we lost most of our tactical equipment. The Cyprian police were augmented by the American Joint Terrorism Task Force in the investigation of the incident. The refueler had been weaponized. Somebody had placed an explosive in the cab of the full fueler. Then they hacked into the brain of the vehicle and drove it via remote control into the hangar. The bomb was detonated by a cell phone signal that was untraceable. It was a complex plan that required somebody skilled enough to hack into the drive-by-wire controls of a Mercedes airport refueling truck, and then to navigate the vehicle across a busy airport using hijacked security cameras as a guide.

The Cyprus police found the person who placed the backpack inside the cab of the truck. It was a middle-aged female airport employee who was blackmailed anonymously over the internet. Somebody had hacked into her phone and threatened to reveal risqué pictures the woman had taken with her gay lover. Rather than expose her indiscretions to a husband and two small children, she opted to cooperate. She claimed she didn't know the small backpack that was delivered to her via courier contained a bomb. She had been told it was drugs that were going to be smuggled onto an aircraft by the refueling crew.

I spent a week alone piloting the *Sam Houston* through the Suez Canal, down the Red Sea, past the Bab al-Mandab Strait, and into the Gulf of Eden. I was through the conflict areas contested by the Iranian-Houthi and Saudi coalition in the narrow strait between Yemen and Africa. It was open sailing to the Gulf of Oman and the Arabian Gulf. Being on the boat alone was a great opportunity for introspection. It was my responsibility to protect my team and I had failed miserably.

I had no idea what I was up against. At this point, I was confident it was more than Prince Turki. The CIA was equally befuddled. It was time to regroup and come up with a plan of attack. I hoped that a revelation would come to me that would allow me to end the madness. I had a conference call scheduled with Cheryl and Mike the next day. The intelligence pros were hard at work doing what they do, which is mostly collecting data and analyzing it. I would be most grateful if one of the big human brains aided by an even bigger computer brain made sense of it all.

I was off the coast of Oman when I dialed into the conference call via satcom. It was 8:00 a.m. in Langley for Mike, 1:00 p.m. for Cheryl in Scotland, and 5:00 p.m. for me. I was inside the wheelhouse, as it was just too hot and muggy outside to pilot from the flybridge.

"Where are you?" Cheryl asked.

"I'm twenty miles off the coast of Muscat. I just refueled."

"Osama Attiyais is off the target list. Change your destination to Abu Dhabi," Mike said.

"Why is that?" I asked.

"The operation was briefed to POTUS and he invited the State Department to opine on the plan. Osama Attiyais is a board member of the Qatar Investment Authority, and they manage three hundred and forty billion dollars in assets. If we grab him it will to too high vis; the White House doesn't want the fallout."

"The White House or the State Department?" I asked.

"State made the recommendation, but the finding to go forward with the operation was pulled by the White House."

"Do we need this Qatari? Where are we on figuring this thing out without him?" I asked. Cheryl cut into the conversation.

"So far, the common thread is the Muslim Brotherhood. Grey Wolves launched the attack in Idlib and seized the Quran. An Egyptian content farm managed an information operation against Saudi Arabia to destabilize it. Qatar is funding at least part of the operation," she said.

"What about Prince Turki; he's not Brotherhood?" asked Mike.

"No, he's not, but because of his experience at the hands of his cousin MBS, he shares a common enemy."

"Have we learned anything from Sahkowi and Zahron?" I asked.

"Yes, a lot. They're the architects of the Saudi rebellion. Both are brilliant social scientists who masterminded an audacious plan to overthrow Saudi. The Qibla controversy was the catalyst, and once they got the protests going, they just built on them by manipulating information. The social media plan they used to generate the unrest is nothing short of genius. Both are now CIA assets."

"Seriously?" I said.

"Yes. What they've done is beyond sophisticated. They turned millions of Saudis into marionettes," Mike said.

"What's going on in Saudi? There's very little on the news," I asked.

"Full-scale civil war. Four different sides are making a run for control," Mike said.

"It's not just the government versus the Wahhabis?" I asked.

"No; once the wheels came off, a group of loyalists to the previous Crown Prince made a move. Prince Abdullah, who commands the Saudi National Guard, has also decided to make a run to be the next King. His father died at the Ritz," he said.

"Did the two Shriners give us any hints on who's calling the shots? Is it Prince Turki or the Qatari?" I asked.

"We don't know for sure, but it may be neither. The cyber-attack and bombing of the Trident facility are way too sophisticated to have come from a Saudi Prince in hiding or a Qatari Investment Authority extremist."

"Who did it, then?"

"We have no idea. The cyber-attack, the bombing, and the manipulation of the social media algos are beyond the known capabilities of the players we have on the table."

"Will Osama Attiyais know the answer?" I asked.

"He may; he's the last clue we have, which is why we wanted to bring him in," Mike said.

"That stinks. What else do we have to talk about?" I asked

"What's your timeline for rebuilding Trident?"

"Six months. Maybe longer, depending on materials. It's going to be expensive and my insurance company is not being very receptive."

"I'll see what we can free up out of the black budget."

CHAPTER 29

Doha, Qatar

I docked the *Sam Houston* at the Ritz Carlton Marina in Doha. I finished tying up the boat and then I walked over to the hotel and checked in. I wasn't going to get any support from Cheryl or Mike on this. Just by being in Doha, I was violating my orders from Mike. Right after our conference call, I went into stealth mode and made sure nothing electronic was telegraphing my location. I knew being off the grid for a day or two would make them suspect that I was in Doha.

My room on the seventh floor had a decent view of the Pearl. The Thabi clan woke up one day and learned that they had twelve trillion dollars in natural gas under the sand of Qatar. Ever since then, they've been desperately trying to buy relevance. Doha embarked on an ambitious plan to match Dubai in the architectural department. Buildings are going up so fast, the skyline changes weekly. The two cities combined have all the culture of a Vegas imitation of a Renaissance city, but that doesn't stop them from trying.

Even though I wasn't going to get any help from either Cheryl or Mike, I still had the target package workup that was sent to me before the abort order. Getting to Osama wasn't going to be easy. The Qatar Investment Authority was a fortress, and his house a palatial dedication to paranoia. My best shot at Osama was going to be a daylight snatch-and-grab while he was on the road going to work.

I spent two days outside his home and his office. His movement patterns were inconsistent. Most people depart and return to work every day at roughly the same time, but Osama was random. He drove around Doha in a chauffeured two-tone white and black Rolls Royce Phantom. Tracking him once he was out and about was never difficult because of the high-profile car. On day three, I decided to make my move. I checked out of the hotel the night before. I moved the *Sam Houston* thirty miles south and anchored two hundred yards off the coast in the town of Mesaleeb. I took my tender and beached on the shore of Mesaleeb and walked a half mile down the road and rented a Chevy Suburban. I drove to Doha and parked where I could see the gated entryway to Osama's mansion. I had no idea when he was going to exit his home and go to work, but since he didn't go to the Qatar Investment Authority yesterday, I was marginally confident he would need to today.

It was almost twelve when I saw the Phantom pass through the black iron gates. It was a Wednesday, and the traffic flow was moderate. I pulled in behind Osama's vehicle and followed. The Rolls stopped at a red light two blocks from his mansion. I waited until the last second to apply my brakes. I skidded briefly and bumped the Rolls from behind. It wasn't hard enough to deploy my airbag, but it was hard enough to dent both of our bumpers. I got out of my car and walked forward as if to survey the damage to my Chevy. Moments later, an Indian driver exited the Rolls and walked back to have a look. Traffic was flowing around our two cars, with the occasional horn honk to express displeasure at the inconvenience we were causing.

"I'm sorry. I accidentally hit the gas instead of the brake," I said to the Indian driver. He just stared at me. "I'll pay for the damage; can I see the owner?" He led me to the Rolls. As I walked, I pulled the Walther PPQ from my back waistband. The rear window of the passenger side of the Phantom rolled down. The tinting was so dark I couldn't see into any of the back windows. While the window was still rolling down, I noticed two people in the rear seat. One was Osama, the second looked like security. I brought the pistol up and fired a single round into the head of the fit-looking man seated next to Osama. The window quickly reversed, and I heard the doors lock. The vehicle was running. I stepped over to the driver's side and fired a bullet into the window and punched my fist through the shattered glass and unlocked the doors. I aimed the pistol at the Indian driver and told him to get in and drive.

From the passenger seat, I alternated between pointing the pistol at the driver and Osama. When we pulled into the beach parking lot of the Mesaleeb beach, I knocked the driver out with a brutal swipe with the butt of my pistol. Osama was a thin man in his fifties and his eyes were round with terror. He wasn't leaving the security of the vehicle without a fight; I could see that plainly. I stunned him with a lightning-quick left jab to the jaw, then I jumped out of the passenger seat and opened the rear passenger door. He covered his face expecting another punch but instead, I dragged him out of the vehicle by his feet. On the way out, he twisted his right leg free and landed a solid kick against my upper thigh. I pulled him closer with his left leg and crushed his nose with a straight right. I dragged the unconscious body fifty yards across the sand to the waiting tender. I pushed the boat into the water, started the engine, and headed out to the *Sam Houston*.

I steered the eleven-foot tender onto the stern hydraulic ramp and then elevated it. I dragged Osama onto the stern deck. I used duct tape to bind his hands and feet. I intended to drag him into the salon, but his broken nose was still bleeding badly and I didn't want to make a mess. Instead, I taped him to the stern deck next to the couch. I walked through the sliding doors and the salon on my way to the wheelhouse. I started the engines and headed away from Qatari waters and into UAE territory at thirty knots. I positioned the boat off the coast of Abu Dhabi, equidistant between Iran and UAE. I ate a tuna fish sandwich and diet coke for lunch and went out to the stern to check on my prisoner.

Osama's white kandura was covered with blood. The bleeding from the nose had finally stopped, but there was a lot of swelling. He had a very short razor-cut beard, curly black hair, and a thin face with coal black eyes. Osama had a weak chin, but his teeth were gleaming white and perfect.

"Whatever you're being paid, I'll triple it," was the first thing he said to me.

"I don't want money. Only information," I said.

"Are you going to kill me?" he asked.

"That's up to you."

"I need water."

I went into the galley and returned with a cold bottle of water and poured it into his mouth. His hands were bound behind his back and he couldn't do it himself.

"Promise me that if I give you what you want, you'll let me go."

"If you tell me what I need to know, I'll head back toward Doha and put you out on the tender and you'll be free."

"Deal. Can we go inside and talk?" It was at least one hundred and ten outside and Osama was very uncomfortable. The deck was burning hot. I decided to stay outside. I set up the video function on my iPad, aimed it down at the hogtied Qatari lying on the stern deck and began the interrogation.

"Why is AMS targeting Saudi Arabia?" I asked.

"To overthrow the government," he answered.

"I've already captured and interrogated Sahkowi and Zahron. Know that before you answer this next question. How did you come to work with Prince Turki?"

"I don't know Prince Turki," he answered.

"Who else is involved in the content-farming operation besides Sahkowi, Zahron, and Prince Turki? Where's the platform-level tech support coming from?"

"I don't know what you're talking about. I employed a group of people to broadcast news over social media into Saudi Arabia. It's no different from Radio Free America. I did nothing wrong; it's not illegal. Why are you treating me like this? This is outrageous! I'm a Qatari citizen; who do you think you are?"

"I had hoped we could have a civil discussion and afterwards I could set you free. It's obvious that's not going to be the case. We'll talk later." I went back into the salon and made a list of the questions I wanted Osama to answer. I cooked spaghetti with garlic shrimp and Bolognese sauce for dinner. I opened a bottle of Ruffino Chianti. When I was finished, I went back out to the stern deck. Osama was non-communicative. He was seated with his back to the couch, his knees were bent, and his head was resting against them. I took a piece of twenty-foot line I used to tie down the yacht, and made and end-of-the-line bowline knot and lassoed it around his waist.

"What are you doing?" he asked in a panicky voice.

"I told you before, I need answers and I'm sick of you lying to me." I picked up Osama, lifted him over my head, all one hundred and forty pounds of him, and tossed him as far as I could into the Gulf. I waited thirty seconds and stepped down beside the tender and slowly began pulling on the line. It didn't take long before I had Osama's panicked, drowning body back onto the hydraulic lift.

After two swims, Osama became a chatty Kathy; he talked so much, I could hardly shut him up. After he had answered all of my questions, I debated shooting him, but ultimately decided against it. There was no tactical benefit gained from killing the Qatari. His testimony made it clear he was a minion doing the bidding of the Qatari national leadership and I thought it would give me an advantage if the Qataris knew that the secret was out. My identity was going to be discovered anyway. I knew that when I'd let the driver live and snatched Osama in a public setting. I took the boat back to the border between Qatar and UAE and sent Osama on his way with my tender back to Doha.

I set a heading for the Yas Marina in Abu Dhabi. I downloaded the video of Osama's interrogation to my Mac and sent an encrypted link of it to Mike and Cheryl. I'm sure Mike was going to hit the roof when he learned of what I had done. I've never been able to understand why Mike chooses to work inside the DC Beltway with the swamp creatures and the constant treachery. Mike will, I'm sure, take a beating because his contractor violated a direct order, but his opponents in the State Department were going to have a lot more to explain because according to Osama, some of them were up to their necks in a conspiracy to overthrow the King of Saudi Arabia.

CHAPTER 30

Abu Dhabi, UAE

It was early morning when I tied down to a slip at the Yas Marina. It was lunchtime when the UAE customs agents finally got around to inspecting my boat. I walked over to the neighboring Viceroy Hotel in the fiery summer afternoon heat. The Viceroy has a unique curved glass design, which to me looks like it was inspired by the shape of a snail. The hotel straddles the Abu Dhabi Formula 1 racetrack and the Yas Marina. I managed to get a room overlooking my boat, and then I headed to lunch at the nearby Crown Plaza to meet with Migos at the Stills Bar.

Stills advertises itself as having the longest bar in Abu Dhabi, which seems a poor indicator of a bar's quality. It's a gastropub with a menu that's familiar to most Americans. I had a draft Stella and the blackened Norwegian Salmon. Migos had a rib eye and a bottle of Heineken. Looking across the table at him, it was obvious the sparkle and the usual levity were missing. He was taking the loss of Jankowski and Burnia very hard. Migos and I had been friends and teammates for a long time. The reason I didn't take him with me to Doha was because I wanted to keep my distance from him. He and I deal with loss very differently. I try my best to ignore it, while Migos does the opposite. He dwells on the subject, constantly injecting it into conversations to the point where it makes me crazy. He's an extrovert who, I'm sure, scores very high in those emotional IQ self-tests you find in magazines; me, not so much.

"Did you grab Osama?"

"Yeah, I did."

"Is the agency sweating him?"

"No, I handled the interrogation myself and then I let him go."

"Why didn't you hand him over?"

"Mike terminated the op while I was still on the way to Doha."

"Why?"

"Politics; the State Department didn't want to offend our friends in Qatar."

"You did it anyway?"

"Yes, to hell with the State Department."

"What did Mike have to say about that?"

"I don't know. I sent him a copy of the interrogation video and haven't heard from him."

"You're in big trouble, aren't you?"

"Probably; definitely, if I didn't get anything worthwhile from Osama. But the residents of Camp Swampy can't defend Qatar on this one. Osama is on the board of the Qatar Investment Authority and he confessed to using his fund to sponsor the Muslim Brotherhood and some other lesser known, but much deadlier, groups. The Qataris' blood feud with Saudi has Americans paying six bucks a gallon for gas. Nobody in DC is going to defend that."

"You're expecting forgiveness, then."

"I'm hopeful, but I sent the video eight hours ago, and up until now nobody's contacted me, so maybe I should be expecting a visit from a wet team instead."

"Did you get any closer to learning who killed our guys?"

"Whoever it is, Osama wasn't dealing with them directly. Hopefully, Clearwater or the Agency analysts can figure something out. Osama threw out a lot of names."

"It really sucks that you couldn't hand him over to the professionals. Nothing personal, but a short field interrogation can't produce anything close to the results of a long stay at a black site."

"I play the cards I'm dealt. Handing him over to the agency wasn't an option. I left him alive, but I wouldn't be surprised if the Qataris end him to cover their tracks."

"Washington almost ruined our chances of finding Burnia and Jankowski's killers. You made the right call."

"I hope Mike sees it that way."

"You should've taken me with you."

"If I didn't get evidence that Osama and his masters were guilty of something much worse than running a content farm, I'd be in even worse trouble than I'm already in. I didn't see any point in bringing company to face a firing squad."

"I'd believe that if you got the abort signal before you headed out solo. Next time, include me." I smiled at that. I really am a terrible liar.

"You can't beat yourself up about what happened in Paphos and you can't do things alone because you don't want to get anyone else hurt," Migos said.

"Here's to Patton, Dornan, Jankowski, and Burnia," I said. We clinked glasses.

"Feel like getting drunk?"

"I wish, but I'm expecting to be called on the carpet at any moment."

CHAPTER 31

Eleuthera, Bahamas

I landed on a charter at Governors Harbor Airport in Eleuthera. It was a short hop from Miami, where I'd landed on the flight from Dubai. Cheryl met me inside the tiny terminal building after Milly, the smiling Bahamian customs lady, stamped my passport at the counter. Cheryl was wearing white shorts and a turquoise blue button down that was the same color as the water surrounding the island. I gave her a hug; her hair smelled like cinnamon. Brilliant conversationalist and seducer of woman that I am, I said:

"You smell like cinnamon."

"I've been baking."

"Are we going to have Chinese cinnamon buns?"

"Pinoy cinnamon rolls. Maria is teaching me how."

"Barefoot and in the kitchen. My dream girl comes to life." She elbowed me as I loaded my luggage in the truck.

"Is Mike at the house?"

"Yes, he got in last night."

"You two had time to talk."

"Yes, for hours."

"Is he after blood?"

"He's calmed down. You put him in a bad position."

"Our whole team was in a bad position when the hangar was attacked. I'm not that sympathetic."

"Don't say that to him. He's always had your back; don't think he doesn't feel just as bad as everyone else about what happened."

"Good advice. I'll take it."

We found Mike sitting on the couch in my office on the top floor. He stood up and we shook hands. He sat back down. I walked to the picture window on the eastern wall. I picked up the binoculars on the window sill and studied the conditions. I hadn't checked the surf report before flying; the swells were at least eight feet. My plans for the day just changed.

Maria brought in a coffee service. Cheryl was sitting away from the coffee table in my favorite Eames lounge chair facing the picture window with her feet up. Mike was back on the couch. I sat in a winged chair across from him.

"Cheryl, Mike's going to yell at me. Do you think you should be here while the boss gives me a reprimand?"

"It's OK if she stays," Mike said. Something was up. Cheryl is the most considerate person in the world, and she wouldn't be sticking around for what I thought should be a one-on-one situation. It was too far out of character.

"Back in the old days, when Dulles was the CIA Director and men were men, we'd be drinking scotch, smoking cigarettes, and before the business talk would begin, I'd get to tap Cheryl on her shapely derrière and say something chauvinistic like, '*run along darling, man talk.*'"

"From what I've noticed, it's more likely she'd do that to you," Mike said.

"I've completely lost control," I said.

"Neutered is the better description," Mike replied.

"Why no angry words about going maverick?"

"You think, after all these years, I didn't know what you were going to do after I cancelled the op? If I really wanted to stop you, I would've sent the Navy and stopped you."

"The abort call was just for CYA purposes then."

"I work in Washington. Of course it was for CYA purposes; I was following orders." I looked over at Cheryl.

"That evil Chinese spy made me think I was going to be in trouble when I reported to the principal's office."

"She's devious."

"Yes, she is."

"She's also very clever."

"And good looking."

"Let's go back to the clever. Cheryl may have figured out who killed our guys." I spilled a little of my coffee. I put the cup and saucer I was holding onto the table.

"Why don't you two tell me what's going on. I don't like secrets; this whole 'I know something you don't know' stuff pisses me off. I sent both of you the video as soon as I had it, so you would be up to date on the operator side. I shouldn't be forced to wait and suffer this theater from the analyst side."

"Pat, if I told you who was responsible while you were in Abu Dhabi, you and Migos would be parachuting in, guns blazing. right now."

"That's a possibility."

"This target will take more finesse than a daylight frontal assault."

"Why is that?"

"Because our target is an American, and not just any American. He's one of the most widely recognized figures in the world. He's revered as a visionary, humanitarian, environmentalist and, potentially, the savior of the species."

"Savior of the species?" I asked.

"He owns a space company that's going to colonize Mars."

"I guess it wouldn't do for it to get out that a CIA contractor hacked his head off with a broadsword."

"Broadsword?"

"I've been toying around with different options for avenging my team."

"Cheryl made the breakthrough. I'll let her bring you up to date."

She sat up on her chair and spun it in our direction. "David Forrest and I received your video. We spent hours researching the people and organizations mentioned by Osama. ALICE is fully back online and he tasked the machine to help.

"We refined our search further. We set out to discover if any of the other Qataris Osama identified as having knowledge of his involvement with the Egyptian content farm also had any connections to the social media platforms that were filtering and distorting the message traffic.

"The QIA is not heavily invested in the US. Their holdings total less than thirty-five billion dollars and they're mostly real estate and not tech investments. We shifted our focus to the personal holdings of the QIA board members. All of them are very wealthy individuals, billionaires without exception. This led us to Abdullah bin Nassar bin Khalifa. Abdullah was involved with Osama's efforts in Egypt and he owns forty percent of a private equity fund headquartered in San Francisco.

"Cascadia Capital has ownership stakes in all of the major internet companies. Everything they have is below the 10 percent SEC reporting requirement, but we were still able to find it."

"How?" I asked.

"ALICE hacked the Cascadia servers."

"The ownership stakes in Alphabet, Facebook, Twitter, and Snapchat turned out to be a dry hole. The one holding that stood out the most in Cascadia's books wasn't a stock holding at all; it's a loan. Cascadia owns seventeen billion of Volta's massive sixty-two-billion-dollar debt.

"We looked further, and we discovered the seven owners of Cascadia are all Qataris. Then we started looking into any connections with Evan Moskowitz. This is where it gets interesting. The largest bondholder of Volta's debt is Cascadia. The second largest bondholder is another private equity company that is owned by a holding company that is owned by Prince Turki from Saudi Arabia. Both Cascadia and Turki obtained their stake after Prince Turki was released from prison in Riyadh. This was a time when Volta was having huge recall issues, production problems, and stories of an impending bankruptcy were a daily feature in the trade news."

"Ok, so you can tie Prince Turki, Abdullah, and Moskowitz together financially. How does that prove anything?" I asked.

"Turki and Abdullah bailed out Volta when nobody else would. Both Turki and Abdullah are already known to be behind the attacks against the Saudi government—Turki through the Turks, and Abdullah through the Egyptians. Between the two of them, they own Evan Moskowitz. The question is, what did they do with that control?

"Moskowitz programmed the computer code that was the foundation for creating the biggest internet company in the world. Turki and Abdullah have the capability to get Moskowitz access to the other platforms. He has the motivation, he has the opportunity, and he has the means. Moskowitz has the skill to write software programs that can manipulate social media to subvert the Saudi Government. Dave Forrest and I are convinced he's the guy who hacked into and ransomed ALICE and the guy who hacked the fuel truck that blew up our hangar and killed our guys."

"And you believe he did all of this to save his own company, Volta?" Mike asked.

"We do," Cheryl said.

"I think I should pay him a visit. Drop by his house, have a beer and maybe ask him a few questions," I said.

"This is why we're having this conversation in person. Murdering Mother Teresa back in her heyday would've generated a smaller public outcry than executing Evan Moskowitz. I aborted the Osama op with a nod and a wink. This is different; I'll need to consult with the Director and he'll need to consult with the DNI, and probably the President. We have to probe Moskowitz very carefully; we can't leave any evidence pointing back to the CIA. We have to be one hundred and ten percent sure he's guilty before we do anything. This is a time for extraordinary caution. Don't—I repeat don't—do anything toward Evan Moskowitz without my approval."

"Gotcha. What about the platforms? Have you at least notified the internet companies, and informed them that their platforms have been compromised and are killing tens of thousands of people each week?"

"We notified them weeks ago, before we ever had any idea who was doing it. Since the problem persists, it's obvious the companies don't know how to stop it. Until we proved to them what was going on, they wouldn't act, because they couldn't even detect it."

"How is that even possible?"

"The internet is incredibly complex. It's like a living organism; there's a lot of hardware and software between the user who receives a message and the platform that message is created on. It could be the manipulation isn't even done on the platforms."

"We need to force Moskowitz to shut down the manipulation."

"Yes, we do."

"And there's nothing they can do in the meantime?"

"They're actively countering the problem with stealth bans and other tools at their disposal. They can only partially mitigate because they're unable to identify and fix the root cause of the problem."

"Is that making a difference on the ground in Saudi?"

"Yes, a lot, but it's going to take months for the flames of revolution to burn themselves out. The House of Saud is not very popular at the moment, but Langley predicts they'll hold on to control."

"What do we do now?"

"Let's focus on finding Turki and proving the case against Moskowitz."

"Marathon analysis sessions with computers and whiteboards, that's just what I wanted to hear," I said. Cheryl got up from her chair and came over to where I was sitting and offered me her hand. I stood up and she reached over and patted me on the backside. "Run along darling, intelligence talk." That made us all laugh.

What Mike said made a lot of sense. But it was frustrating to hear; the last thing I wanted was for the government to turn the case against Moskowitz into a criminal matter. I decided to go surfing and rushed downstairs to get changed.

Later, the three of us went into Governors Harbor for dinner. 1648 is a restaurant on the edge of town on a cliff overlooking the Caribbean. The food is excellent, but not nearly as good as the view. We sat outside. I ordered an Island Pirate Ale IPA. I was a little dehydrated from my exertions in the surf.

"I think we need to be realistic about Moskowitz," Mike said, as I was piling my plate with appetizers. I had a solid base of shrimps and crab cakes and was adding the conch Rangoons.

"You mean the US government is never going to greenlight a hit on their wonder boy," I said.

"Yeah. That's a definite possibility. We have enough that the Feds will put him under a microscope—FISA, the whole business—but it's unrealistic to expect that if the government moves against him, it will be anywhere but through the courts."

"And in the courts, they won't charge him for the murder of covert members of a CIA sponsored black cell that exists to skirt congressional oversight," I said.

"Right, and unless he hacked into Facebook or one of the other companies directly and we can prove it, which so far we can't, I'm not sure he can be charged with anything."

"The guy's a menace; he sounds like one of those megalomaniacs who thinks he's a god and can do whatever he pleases. It's not a good idea to let him run free. Next time, he's liable to cause a war between US and Russia instead of merely sending the global economy into a tailspin by fermenting a revolution in Saudi. Let me handle it. I'll make it look like an accident."

"An accident; seriously?"

"They have a lot of bears in Washington State. He could be attacked by one in his kitchen. Bear claw marks can look surprisingly like the blade cuts from a broadsword by the way."

"That's not funny."

"None of this is funny and I'm uncertain if I see a point in going after Turki. His motivation I understand."

"The slaughter of the archaeologists in Syria is not to be forgiven."

"That was Omar. Turki didn't come into the picture until later."

"We don't know that. I haven't heard a lot lately about the lost Quran and the new Qibla in the media. Is that controversy dying down?"

"That's what we have Sahkowi and Zahron working on. They're dissecting a translated copy you took of the book from Omar and we're using their Arab social science magic and a content farm of our own to discredit the book and shift the faithful back to Mecca."

"Surf season will be peaking for the next three months. I'm going to stay here in the Bahamas and let you Machiavelli the world back to normal."

"About that; I've been talking to Cheryl about coming to Langley for a while." I looked over at Cheryl. She looked embarrassed by the news.

"I'm not saying this for selfish reasons, although I do hate the idea on that level. It's not safe for Cheryl to be overtly working with the

CIA. To me and you she's Cheryl. We used to know her as Susu. But to the Chinese Intelligence, she's Colonel Shu Xue Wong, and if they ever discover she's alive, they're going to kill her in the most painful way possible. To them, she's a traitor who betrayed Chinese intelligence, staged her death, and defected to the enemy. This is why she should keep a low profile and stay in Paphos or in Eleuthera under my personal protection."

"You guys are talking about me like I'm not even here," Cheryl said.

"Langley is a bad idea, I said."

"We can offer protection; it won't be any less safe than here," Mike offered.

"Let me think about it."

"It's not your choice, Pat; it's mine, and I'm going. Dave and I have developed an important capability that's needed at Langley. We found out the hard way in Paphos that it needs to be properly protected. It won't be forever."

"Do you two have any more bad news for me?" I signaled the waitress and ordered another beer.

"I've already reviewed a list of candidates for you to consider. I'm going to send it to you, so can start doing interviews and begin to rebuild your team."

"It's difficult to take advice on replacing Burnia and Jankowski, guys who gave everything, from the same people who are protecting their killer."

"That's not fair."

"There are a lot of things in life that are unfair. But that doesn't make them less true."

CHAPTER 32

Seattle, Washington

Evan Moskowitz walked out of the helicopter and headed to the door that led down into his office. The roar of the rotor blades was deafening. Tabitha, his personal assistant, met him at the entrance to the stairwell. She was speaking, but he couldn't hear over the sound of the helicopter. She was tapping her watch, indicating he was late—something he was well aware of. He walked through his office, stopping only long enough to hand his jacket to Tabitha, and breezed into the adjacent conference room.

His meeting was with Derrick Wilson, Volta's government affairs officer and Senator Tim Doorman, a senior partner from a Washington Law Firm that specialized in legislative affairs—in other words, a lobbyist. Having dodged several bullets over the past year, Evan was confident this next one could be managed. The major recall for exploding batteries, the production delays, and the debt crisis were all supposed to bury him, but he was still standing. This next crisis was going to be no different.

Both men stood to greet him as he entered. They all shook hands. Evan waited for Tabitha to serve fresh coffee to the visitors and leave the conference room before getting down to business.

"Sorry I'm late; I got caught up with something. Let's get right to the point. If they took the vote today, where would we stand?" Evan asked the former Senate Whip.

"In the House, we have the votes. The problem is in the Senate. We need to flip two votes."

"What about the President?"

"He'll sign the bill if it gets to him. Three German companies are entering the US electric car market next year. Stopping the sunset of the individual car subsidy helps his case in the upcoming trade negotiations with the EU. It gives him a bargaining chip he can use," the Senator replied.

"Give me a list of the names of the Senators you expect to vote against the bill," Evan stated. The Senator had a complete report with all of the names as well as suggested talking points for an engagement strategy with each one. He handed a bound presentation to both Evan and his VP for Government Affairs, expecting a lengthy strategy session to follow.

"Thank you, gentlemen, for your time," Evan said

Armed with a list of fifty-one names, Evan went directly to his office desk and went to work. The two visitors said their goodbyes on the way out, but he didn't hear them because he was already lost in thought. He worked at a manic pace for two straight days with hardly a break. He didn't sleep, and he didn't eat. A steady diet of cocaine and coffee kept him energized. When he finally finished his task, he rubbed the stubble on his chin and ordered a company plane to fly him to Butte, Montana. Then he crashed on his office couch.

Storing servers in the cold Rocky Mountain air saved Evan millions in cooling costs; miles and miles of server racks generate a lot of heat. SysData Storage was Evan's most neglected holding. He rarely visited the SysData Storage complex because of its out-of-the-way location, and because he found data storage to be an intensely boring subject. His only fondness for the business came from the steady income it generated. Most of the revenue came from performing data storage for big insurance companies and government agencies— organizations that generate mountains of documents that need to be digitized, retrievable, and retained for long periods. One of those agencies was the FBI. Over the past two days, he'd completed a lifestyle profile on every Senator who was expected to vote against extending the tax credit. He narrowed the fifty-one names down to eleven targets. He focused on those eleven targets and identified specific time periods for each individual where he would concentrate his search. He was sure he'd find what he needed on at least two of the Senators. He had a lot of reasons to be confident. He had access to every FBI case file and report ever submitted, and he was a computer genius who could sift through those files at lightning speed and find what he needed.

The FBI server farm is a highly secure facility. It can't be accessed by the internet. Its only external connection is to the FBI headquarters, and that's by a secure fiber optic link. To access the files, a person needs to be physically present at the server farm in Montana or in the Hoover building in DC. Evan could never access the info through FBI channels, but as the owner of SysData Storage, he had a free pass to the server farm any time he wanted.

He was met at the Butte Airport by the facility General Manager. The reason he gave for his visit was a data compression upgrade he was working on. The reason for the visit, as flimsy as it was, went unquestioned. He was Evan Moskowitz, a deity to people in the tech community. He could have told the GM the real purpose for his visit and it would have been met with unquestioned support. The highlight of the GM's career, perhaps even his life, would be the day he escorted Evan Moskowitz from the airport to the server farm.

It took him only five hours alone behind a computer console to get what he needed. He made sure to erase any trace of his activity. Connections to the system with a USB or a printer would have raised an alarm to the FBI, who monitored all access to the system. He captured screenshots of the documents he needed from the monitor screen using his cell phone.

He met his personal lawyer and fixer at his office in Seattle before heading to San Francisco for the weekend. His lawyer would engage a security firm they used occasionally to solve sensitive issues. An ultimatum would be passed to the targeted Senators early the next week. Given the choice between either saving the environment by voting to extend a $7,500 tax credit on electric vehicles, or losing their next reelection bid because of a scandal, Evan was certain the decision would be easy.

Evan dressed for the charity dinner in the tux Tabitha laid out for him and had a car take him to the airport. His girlfriend met him in a limo at the Palo Alto Airport private terminal, and after receiving a humanitarian award at the Annual San Francisco GLAAD gala, he spent the weekend partying with his popstar girlfriend and her friends. By Thursday the next week, he received confirmation the approach to the Senators had been made. The first target, the Senior Senator from

Alaska, had agreed to the proposition on the spot. The response of the second target, the Senior Senator from Georgia, had been puzzling, to say the least.

Senator Raymond Childers was elected to the Senate in 1994. He was a prominent Republican with a strong conservative voting record. He was a family man with a wife and two adult children. Prior to entering the Senate, he was a popular Congressman and, before that, Childers was a high school teacher. During an annual week-long school trip to Italy while still a teacher, Senator Childers became romantically involved with his Italian guide. Months later, after Childers ignored attempts from the young lady to communicate with him, the girl, out of frustration, visited the US Embassy in Rome and requested assistance in reaching Childers.

Many years later, when Senator Childers was getting his background investigation for his Top Secret security clearance, the investigators found the Italian girl's inquiry in the State Department records. The investigators also discovered a payment of $100,000 to the girl many years later. The investigators learned the payment was consideration exchanged for the signing of a non-disclosure agreement. The protected information the agreement was created to keep secret was the fact that Childers had impregnated the Italian girl and later paid for an abortion.

Impregnating girls and paying for abortions are not crimes. The concern of the security clearance background investigators was restricted to the threat of blackmail from the girl. The existence of an NDA was found to provide sufficient protection and a Top Secret/Special Background Investigation security clearance was granted. The file was closed and never re-opened.

Evan couldn't understand why the Senator didn't jump at the deal. As one of the most vocal pro-life candidates in the country, it made no sense that he was willing to risk exposure as a hypocrite instead of voting for a tax credit that would go largely unnoticed by his supporters. He called his fixer and asked him to meet, so he could pass him the information on the third target; his backup was a Senator from New Mexico. He thought the Senator from Georgia would eventually come around, but it never hurt to have a fallback plan.

160

CHAPTER 33

Eleuthera, Bahamas

We were midway through hurricane season the next time the subject of Evan Moskowitz came up. Cheryl was experiencing autumn in Northern Virginia, and I was living on the beach in Eleuthera. We traded visits every other weekend. She was working marathon hours while I was mostly just hanging out at the beach.

Mike popped down to Eleuthera for a visit. I was guessing he was just checking in on me because he gave no reason for coming. I still hadn't hired replacements for the guys we lost in Paphos. The reconstruction of the Paphos hangar was almost complete, but my heart wasn't into the act of rebuilding the team.

He came early, after I was just finishing up my morning surf. I was still in my wetsuit on the second-floor sun deck when Maria opened the porch door and let him through. He sat in the wicker chair next to mine. I was drinking coffee, weary and sore from spending the previous three hours battling the waves. The deck is a wrap around, with a view of both oceans. We were looking out on the Atlantic side; the weather was cloudy, and a blustery wind was coming in from the ocean. The surf was rough; a tropical storm was generating big swells that made for an exciting morning.

"How are David and Cheryl coming along?" I asked.

"Good. When they're done, ALICE will live in our computer facility in Fredericton, but David will have remote access from Scotland and Paphos."

"Is that all there is to his system, the AI driven computer?"

"No, it's much more than that. It's the way ALICE synchronizes with the sensors. Cheryl has a better understanding of sensors, and

David is the computer whiz. Together they've pioneered some techniques that they're sharing with our people in-house."

"How can ALICE be used for commercial purposes if it's owned by the government? We make a pretty good business tracking, and sometimes finding, maritime assets for shippers and insurance companies," I said.

"The system belongs to Clearwater; we're keeping it in Virginia to safeguard it, is all."

"I have no objections. I just don't want you to wind up in a congressional oversight hearing about it."

"No danger there."

"Speaking of congressional oversight, that's why I'm here." My ears perked up at that.

"Our boy Evan can't seem to color inside of the lines. The tax bill last year cut out the subsidy for electric cars. Uncle Sam's $7,500 represents a pretty big discount, and without it, his sales are going to take a pretty big hit."

"Go on. I'm listening."

"He paid a leg breaker to approach Senator Childers and offer him silence on an indiscretion involving an abortion he paid for years ago, in exchange for a yes vote on the upcoming bill stopping the sunsetting of the electric car tax credit."

"How do you know he did that?"

"Hubris. The guy was so confident Childers would take the deal and keep his mouth shut, he used a law firm to hire the thug that, after only a little research, traced all the way back to Moskowitz. Childers has stage four lymphoma; he's dying and couldn't care less about reelection. His wife knows about the girl and the abortion, so his only vulnerability is the voters which matter very little at this point in his political career. He's kept his diagnosis secret and Moskowitz knew nothing about it. We got lucky because after he was contacted, Childers went straight to the FBI and from there it took less than a week to connect the dots back to the law firm, and back to Moskowitz."

"Moskowitz being a bad guy has already been established."

"This is a new level. He's gone beyond meddling in the affairs of Saudi Arabia. He's now stealing secrets from the FBI and blackmailing US Senators."

"Have the powers that be decided to do something about it?"

"I had a very private meeting with the Director and the DNI. Moskowitz has the contract managing the servers for the FBI, HSA, ATF, as well as other agencies not connected to national security. These facilities are supposed to be secure, and the data within them not accessible by the hosting company. Moskowitz found a way to bypass that security. The top FBI computer experts can't find any evidence that Moskowitz got the info to blackmail Childers from the FBI, but given his talent in the area, we believe that's where the dirt on Childers came from."

"How does any of this involve me and Trident?"

"It doesn't involve Trident at all."

"Now you have me confused."

"Let me explain. Moskowitz has the head of the FBI and President himself terrified. He's out of control, completely off the rails; he's willing to do anything to get what he wants, and he has billions of dollars and access to many of the Nation's most closely guarded secrets at his disposal. Moskowitz can no longer be trusted. By accessing the FBI files, he's become a clear and present danger."

"Why doesn't the FBI arrest him?"

"The firm that made the approach to Childers has worked in the past for Moskowitz. That's all the evidence against him. We can't prove he accessed the FBI data, and unless the goon who threatened Childers flips on him, we can't prove Moskowitz was involved at all."

"Maybe he's not involved?"

"No chance. He's involved, and if we go after him in the courts, he's going to beat the charge, and for all we know he's got the dirt on many more public officials and politicians."

"That's a problem. Why would the FBI hand over all of their secrets to a dotcom billionaire anyway?"

"Dotcom billionaires are the only people with the skills and resources to manage big data. Do you know who handles the CIA's servers?"

"No, who?"

"Jeff Bezos from Amazon, who's also the owner of the Washington Post." That made me chuckle.

"I'm sure you have nothing to worry about with that choice. What's the plan on Moskowitz?"

"The FBI is going to quietly investigate. In the cloak and dagger meeting I had with the DNI, his exact words were 'If someone were to take Moskowitz out they'd be doing all of us a huge favor.' I told him that Moskowitz had plenty of enemies, but nobody that was going to solve our problem for us. His response was that he wouldn't be surprised if Pat Walsh went after him. He said you've never been one to listen to orders." I paused for a few seconds while I processed what he said.

"That's the King Henry, 'Will nobody rid me of this turbulent priest?' defense. He gave the order without giving the order. That's a pretty gutless way to authorize an operation, if you ask me."

"Welcome to the world of Washington. It's an unsanctioned operation; if you get caught, you're on your own and nobody can help. Once he's dead, nobody's going to look very hard to find out who did it."

"That works for me."

"On your own Pat; no Trident assets either."

"Do you want me to recover the information he stole from the FBI, or is this just a hit?"

"We'd love to know how he's manipulating the social media, and what other FBI files he has. But this is improv, and we don't expect miracles."

"How many people know I've been given the green light?"

"You, me, and the Director of National Intelligence, for sure. I would guess the President has a good idea what's going on. The DNI is not one to operate without top cover."

"Small group. Let's keep it that way."

"Best if you make it look like an accident or natural causes, but nobody's too worried about the how; he just needs to be taken off the board. Maybe you can do something with his growing drug habit." He handed me a thick manila envelope.

"What's this?"

"A target folder. Burn it when you're done with it. It has everything we know about his habits, movements, and security."

"Cool. Are you hungry? Feel like wandering over to Tippy's bar and having a beer and grouper sandwich?"

We walked next door and had a terrific lunch. After I've been in the salty ocean water for hours, beer tastes so much better. After lunch, Mike flew back to Langley and I retreated to my office to study the target.

CHAPTER 34

Seattle, Washington

I drove off the Bainbridge Island Ferry in my rental and headed north on Alaska to the Seattle Marriott. I went to the island to see if it was a feasible starting point to surveil Evan. It wasn't; his home on Bainbridge Island couldn't have been less suitable.

Evan has a sprawling estate on the Puget Sound shoreline. It's a beautiful stone house facing the Olympic Mountains to the west and is surrounded by a forest of hundred-foot evergreens. I drove by his house, but my only information on what his actual residence looks like came from magazine articles. He has an iron gate blocking the access road to his house and a forest concealing it from the road. A hundred acres normally buys a guy a lot of privacy and gives someone like me a few quality scouting options. Unfortunately, in Evan's case, the combination of the local culture, his high-tech smart-home, and a full-time personal security detail makes surveillance of his house too difficult.

I expect billionaires to have personal security details; if they didn't they'd get kidnapped and used as ATMs. Evan has a PSD that stays with him whenever he goes out in public. From media searches, I could see that he always has at least two members of his PSD with him. The existence of a permanent detail at his house is just a guess. I found a lot of information on his home by doing a web search; his place had been featured a several magazine articles and even a TV show. It's a seventy-five-million-dollar high tech smart home with a state-of-the-art security system.

Making matters worse is the local culture. Bainbridge is an ultra-community-conscious island neighborhood where everybody knows each other. The level of community awareness borders on intrusive.

It's not the kind of place you can park a car on a road and leave it for a few days while you go out to conduct a recon. It's more like the kind of place where people check each other's trash to make sure they're recycling and only eating organic. There's not a single franchise store on the island, and the hotels are all small inns or bed-and-breakfasts. It's a virtue-signaling heaven, and a terrible place to find the kind of anonymity I need to work. Despite his near-god status as a death dealer to the combustion engine and the evil oil industry, Evan's neighbors complain about him constantly. I read through back issues of the local paper, the *Bainbridge Review*, and found half a dozen complaints on the noise pollution created by his frequent helicopter use. I ruled out Bainbridge pretty quickly. The only benefit from my trip was the nice scenery on the ferry ride from Seattle.

Evan's office was equally problematic. Volta doesn't have a lone office building in the downtown with public access, but instead has a secure campus on the north side of the city. Industrial espionage from competitors and bad actors like China have made tech companies hyper-vigilant. The security at most high-tech firms is better than at most US military installations. Volta was no exception; access was closely controlled, and cameras were everywhere.

Work and home were out. I needed to get to Evan when he was out and about, and to do that, I needed advance knowledge of where he was going, or I needed to find a way to put a tracker on him. I really missed having a team to support me. That's what I was thinking about as my head hit the pillow on the bed in the Marriott.

After a quick nap, I walked down the street to Anthony's Pier 66. Seattle's downtown has more than its fair share of excellent restaurants. Anthony's isn't one of them. I chose it because it's big and busy, and I knew I wouldn't be remembered. The weather was overcast with a mild drizzle. I came to Seattle prepared. I had plenty of experience staying wet for weeks at a time in the woods during my junior officer days in the Second Ranger Battalion at nearby Fort Lewis. I was seated next to the window, eating hot clam chowder, looking out at the ferry terminal, when the idea hit me.

Evan was cocooned by security. His house and office were high-tech fortresses. Without support from Clearwater or the Agency, I had no way of obtaining advance knowledge of Evan's schedule or tracking his movements. The one thing I did know about his movements was his reliance on a helicopter to travel to and from work. Relying on a helicopter means he's also reliant on the weather and Seattle weather was guaranteed to force him to occasionally have to cancel his air travel. I wondered what he did when the weather was bad? Did he work from home? Did he use the ferry, or did he use whatever he had in that boathouse I saw a picture of in the magazine article? I decided to find out what was in that boathouse.

The next morning, I traded my rental Subaru in for a Suburban. Then I went to REI and bought a dark green kayak and a wetsuit. Next, I hit the road. The drive to the tiny town of Brownsville, which is across the water from the Venice area of Bainbridge Island, took an hour and a half. I put the kayak in the water at Brownsville public pier and paddled north up the narrow waterway of Port Orchard. There was a gentle rain with only a light wind. The air temperature was fifty-five degrees, and the water temperature about the same. It took me forty-five minutes to paddle to Evan Moskowitz's house. I wasn't the only killer in the water this morning. The Sound was teaming with sea life. An orca sounded less than fifty yards off my port side, its black and white pattern standing out in contrast to the dark blue water and the lush evergreen background. For most of the trip, I was followed by a playful pair of harbor porpoises and the barking of seals was nonstop.

I slowed when I reached the boathouse, which was connected to the property edge by a small wooden pier. The boathouse door was closed, and I couldn't see inside. I paddled in closer to the shore and was able to catch a glimpse of the boat through a side window. Based on the dimensions of the boathouse and what little I see through the window, my best guess was what he had inside was a thirty-to-forty-foot cabin cruiser. Given his money, I was sure it would be fast. I loitered until I saw a door open in the house and a security guard emerge. That was my cue to move on. I couldn't see any cameras on the boathouse or the dock, but there must have been some or the guard wouldn't have come out. I continued to paddle north another mile up to the Agate Passage Bridge and then turned around and made my way back. The waterway narrows to only a hundred and fifty yards from shore to shore at the bridge and then opens up again. In a commute to his campus in northern Seattle, the shortest route for Moskowitz would be north past the bridge. My reconnaissance confirmed the plan I had mulling around in my head. All I had to do now was secure some equipment. I came to Seattle on a private charter, so I could bring a few weapons and explosives. To complete the rest of the kit I needed, I would have to go shopping on the local market.

I rented some scuba gear and drove back to Brownsville to make a night dive. I waited until midnight before stepping off the pier. The cold water shocked my system. Eventually, the wet suit and the heat generated from the swim warmed me up. I snorkeled for half a mile until I spotted the lights from Evan's house. I spit out the snorkel, inserted my regulator, eased the air out of my buoyancy compensator, and slipped under the surface. I kept my depth to only a few feet below the surface. I didn't use a flashlight, and the overcast sky made for a very dark diving experience. I swam toward the lone illuminated window in Evan's house. I lost the light when I got close to the boat house and was just about to surface to get my bearings when I bumped into the hull of Evan's boat.

I surfaced inside the boat garage, between the bow of the boat and the closed garage door. I removed the adhesive backing from a small RFID tracker I carried in the pocket of my BCD. It was hard to handle the tracker wearing neoprene gloves in the dark, but I managed. I reached up and attached the tracker high on the bow of Moskowitz's thirty-six-foot Chris Craft Corsair. The tracker was placed just below the top lip and wouldn't be visible from the deck. Once it was attached, I depressed the rubber button on the bottom, and it flashed green twice to signal it was on. The tracker would go dormant and wouldn't begin transmitting until the boat moved. I slipped back below the surface and made my way under the garage door and back into the Puget Sound.

I arrived back at the Marriott at five that morning. I took a short nap and then went to work. I returned the scuba gear, and after searching the classifieds, bought a used Jeep and a Jet Ski with cash. I gassed up the Jeep and parked it along my exfil route. I towed the Jet Ski behind my rented Suburban. I did some more shopping at the local hobby store and then checked in at the Suquamish Casino Resort. I picked the hotel because it's only a hundred yards from the Agate Passage Bridge. I was ready; now all I needed to do was wait for bad weather

Over the next week, we had two days where the morning fog was unsafe for helicopter flight. Both days, Moskowitz had either stayed in or used the ferry, because his boat didn't move. The long wait was making my stay at the hotel awkward. The Suquamish Casino Resort ("Truckers Welcome") is not the kind of place people stay for more than a week or two. The tall guy with the wet suit and Jet Ski was starting to raise suspicion, if not as an executioner, at least as a crazy person.

On my ninth morning of water watching, the alarm on my iPad sounded; the RFID tracker was transmitting. I threw a backpack over my shoulder and jogged out to my Jet Ski that the hotel generously allowed me to park on the beach. I dragged the Jet Ski into the water and took off toward the bridge. I moved the Jet Ski into position next to one of the center pillars of the Agate Passage Bridge and tied down. The current was strong, and the rope became taut once I shut the machine off. I placed my iPad on the dash and watched the icon move toward me. I removed the night vision head harness from my backpack and slipped it on. The specs on Moskowitz's boat said it was capable of forty knots. But the fog was so thick, I didn't think they'd be going more than ten or fifteen knots in the narrow waterway. I was counting on them slowing down even more when they approached the bridge.

I slid the blasting cap into the well of the C4 and tied the two loose connections to the electric posts of the RF receiver unit. I started the gas engine on a three-foot-long remote-control boat I'd picked up at a hobby store and rested it on my knee. Moskowitz's boat approached on my iPad tracking app. The map showed the boat only two hundred yards away, the high-pitched noise of the RC boat motor making it difficult for me to hear it approach. I activated a Hot Hands glove warmer by crushing it and slid it under the elastic to keep it secured on the RC boat. I gently placed the RC boat into the water. I picked up the hand-held remote control between my knees and steered the RC into the fog to my front. I dropped the thermal monocular mounted on my night vision harness over my right eye. I had lost the RC boat with my naked eye because of the fog, but once I dropped the thermal I could see a white-hot spot made by the Hot Hands attached to the boat just fine. Evan's cabin cruiser came into view seconds later.

The motor boat was approaching down the center of the waterway. I adjusted the path of the remote control boat a little to the right and put it on course for a collision. I drove the RC boat straight into the bow of the approaching craft. When the two hot spots merged on my thermals, I hit the detonator button on the control unit and sent a radio signal to the RF receiver connected to the elastic blasting cap. The muted explosion from a half block of C4 plastic explosive opened a hole the size of a trap door in the bow of the cabin cruiser's fiberglass hull. The forward speed of the cruiser did the rest.

Within five minutes, only the top of the boat's cabin was visible through my thermals. I started the Jet Ski, untied it from the pillar and approached the wreck. I found three people in the water slowly trying to make it to shore. None of them were wearing life jackets and the freezing cold water was already taking effect. I took the deflated two-man life raft from my backpack. I pulled the igniter, and a CO_2 cartridge inflated the raft forcing it to fall from my hands. I kicked the raft over to the nearest man. He grabbed onto the side rope, the other two men struggling to swim toward the raft in the unbearably cold water. I studied the group. I intercepted the trail swimmer.

"There's not enough room on the raft for three. You can ride with me," I said to the man the farthest from the raft.

He reached out and I pulled him by his arm up onto the jet ski, making sure he was between me and the handle bars. He was shivering so badly his teeth were chattering. From my seat behind him, I stabbed him in the side of the neck with a syrette of Ketamine. In a matter of seconds, he was unconscious. I spun the Jet Ski and turned back to the raft.

"I need to get your friend to a hospital; he's in a bad way." I didn't wait for a response. I hit the gas, and in seconds disappeared in the fog. The men on the raft were trying to tell me something, but I couldn't make out what was being yelled over the roar of the Jet Ski. The nearest help was the Resort I'd been staying at under an alias.

I estimated it would take them ten to fifteen minutes to get there, floating as they were with the current. My transfer point was ten minutes away in Point Wells, just a few miles north of Seattle.

I raced through the fog and beached the Jet Ski next to a parking lot adjacent to a tank farm. I lifted Evan onto my shoulder and hiked up the hill to my waiting 1978 Wagoneer. I cut Moskowitz's clothes off him in case he had a personal locator beacon or an electric device that could be tracked. I laid him flat in the back area of the SUV. I flex cuffed his hands and feet, and threw a wool blanket over him for concealment, and to keep him from dying of hypothermia.

It took ten hours to reach the Airbnb cabin I'd rented for three nights in Sun Valley, Idaho. The mountain cabin was isolated. I was able to check in electronically with a burner phone. Moskowitz had been awake and vocal for the last two hours of the trip; I ran out of Ketamine syrettes in Spokane. I carried him into the dining room and left him on the tile floor. Then I got back in the Jeep and drove two miles back down the mountain to the grocery store we passed on the way up.

I gave Evan a bottle of Ensure.

"Drink this, it'll give you energy and you'll be able to keep it down with the nausea you must be feeling from the drug." I poured half the liter bottle into him. He gulped it down.

"What do you want? Is it money?"

"I don't want money. Our task here is discovery." I set the tripod and camera up.

"You're going to detail everything you did, and everything that needs to be undone to stop the internet manipulation against the government of Saudi Arabia. Passwords, the whole bit. Next, you'll be describing how you got access into the FBI files. What files you took. Where those files are, the works."

"Are you with the government?"

"When we're done with the FBI files, I'll need the names and conditions on all of the people you blackmailed. Finally, I'm going to need to know who else you're working with— Turki, Abdullah, etc. It's going to be a long conversation."

"I want to talk with whomever you're working for. I'm not giving you anything until I speak with the top man and get a guarantee that you'll release me."

"Evan, you're going to give me that information to stop the pain. That's the deal I'm offering you. I get the information I want, and you get to keep your body parts. It's a very straightforward arrangement. Don't overcomplicate it."

"I want to talk with your boss."

Moskowitz was tied to a wooden kitchen chair. His arms and wrists were tied to the arm rests. I reached over and snapped his right index finger. I bent it so far back it touched his wrist. He screamed. That's all it took. Nobody will ever accuse Evan Moskowitz of physical bravery.

The interrogation lasted two full days. Moskowitz had an amazing memory and he was extremely cooperative, almost bordering on being ingratiating. When it was over, we drove north on Highway 21. It was cold in the mountains. There was frost on the road. Moskowitz was still unclothed. He was shaking in the back seat of the truck.

"Where are we going? We had a deal. You were going to let me go," he whimpered.

I didn't say anything. I pulled off onto a logging trail and drove into the woods for another thirty minutes. Moskowitz was screaming and yelling in panic as the truck bumped along the dirt trail. He started to bang his head against the headrest behind him. I opened the back door, pulled him out and threw him onto the ground. I withdrew the HK VP 9 pistol I was carrying in my waistband and aimed it at him. He stopped yelling and froze; he was lying flat on his back looking up at me as I stood over him. I pulled the trigger. The bullet hit where I aimed it—one inch above his forehead. He passed out.

He regained consciousness on the way back to the cottage.

"My name is Pat Walsh, but you already know that. You must have studied my files when you broke into Clearwater. Clever of you not to mention your part in that attack."

"I didn't recognize you. I knew the name Pat Walsh, but there were no images."

"You killed four of my people."

"I'm sorry. I'm really sorry."

"The CIA wants me to kill you. Mostly because the people the CIA reports to want you dead."

"They want me dead?"

"Yeah, you've been very bad. They sent me to kill you. You work for me now."

"I work for you."

"I'm going to let you go, and I'm going to tell the CIA that you're my asset. The next time you step out of line, I won't go through the trouble of kidnapping you. I'll just kill you. You'll never see me coming. Understood?"

"Thank you. Thank you. I won't step out of line. I'll never disappoint you. I promise. Thank you." I looked though the rearview mirror; tears were running down his face.

CHAPTER 35

Abu Dhabi, UAE

Mike and I were seated at the 99 Sushi Bar in the Four Seasons Hotel in Maryah Island, Abu Dhabi. Mike's a foodie and figured if I wowed him with a great dining experience, he'd process his anger all the quicker. He was mad though, about as mad as I've ever seen him.

"This is called haute Japanese cuisine. Its new and you're going to love it. They have a sommelier for sake."

"Sake sounds perfect."

I called the waiter over and told him to get the sake guy. I ordered for both of us. I chose sea urchin, prawns, toro, black cod, steak, and about everything else on the menu. Afterward, I told the sake guy to take his cue from the dishes and surprise us. It was a magnificent meal. We had five different sakes, and the sommelier did an excellent job of explaining each one. It wasn't until we were both feeling good, and about to attack our passion fruit mochi dessert, that the topic of work came up.

"Why did you let Evan go?" he asked.

"Because he beat David Forrest and he did it without a super-computer powered by artificial intelligence. He did it alone, by himself."

"That's what makes him a threat. It's why he had to be dealt with."

"He can be controlled; he was following orders from Turki. Now he works for us."

"Can we control him?"

"I think so. It's worth a shot. If he goes maverick, I'll kill him."

"He killed your guys. Why the compassion.?"

"I'm just being pragmatic. I'm feeling more and more like a dinosaur these days; the future of the business is with the David Forrest and the Evan Moskowitz types. Moskowitz is a horrible person, but you need to have a weapon of his caliber in your pocket or what happened to us in Paphos is going to happen again."

"I'll buy that."

"It's like taking the Nazi scientists after WWII and using them for our space program. We don't have to like these people, we just need to recognize that the opposition is after the same thing and we need parity, or we risk oblivion."

"How sure are you that he's firmly under your control?"

"He's not completely free of his old obligations. Turki and Abdullah still have influence over him, because they're holding thirty-one billion dollars of his paper. We need to remedy that. It was Turki that gave the order for the attack on Paphos. He's the top guy in this conspiracy. Both Turki and Abdullah need to die."

"Abdullah is acting on behalf of the State of Qatar. We'll deal with him differently. Let me handle that one. You find Turki and no more of this catch and release stuff."

"Turki is in Tangier, Morocco."

"Did Evan tell you that?"

"Yes, they communicate through a chat room on a video game. Evan was able to trace him."

"What do you have Evan doing now?"

"He's removing the filters and changing the algos that were distorting the search rankings for the anti-Saudi content, and he's standing by for further instructions."

CHAPTER 36

Tangiers, Morocco

The sail from Paphos to the Gibraltar Strait took a week. We diverted to Spain for a day to take on some gear we were going to need in the mission ahead. Migos, McDonald and I spent some of our time aboard the *Sam Houston* reviewing the replacement candidates for Jankowski and Burnia. We spent the remainder preparing for the operation.

Tangier, Morocco, sits only ten miles off the southern tip of Spain. The narrow waterway between the two land masses of Morocco and Spain is the Strait of Gibraltar. Gibraltar is also the boundary between the Mediterranean and the Atlantic Ocean. It's a busy place for sea transport. We anchored the *Sam Houston* south of the shipping lane and three miles north of Turki's property. It was already dark by the time we reached our destination—too dark to see the cliffs to our south.

Migos and I were in dry suits and closed-circuit dive gear. I had a heavy pack of equipment strapped to my back. On my chest, I was wearing a SIEL rebreather unit with a 240-minute soda lime canister. We bobbed in the gentle sea waiting for McDonald to hand us the Suex Scooters off the hydraulic ramp. Once we had the scooters in hand, we descended to ten feet. Through my mask, I could see the compass and depth gauge illuminated on top of the scooter. My rifle dangled below me on a sling.

I looked around for Migos; it was pitch black, but I felt his scooter bump up against my ribs. The crescent moon provided no visibility at our depth. Migos tapped me on the arm and I eased my scooter to full throttle. He would follow the small green LED light attached to the bottom of my backpack.

We slid through the water at three knots. The speed pressed my mask tight up against my face and made it impossible to turn my head lest the water rip it off. Unable to see anything, I concentrated on the navigation board built into the scooter and maintained a bearing of one hundred and sixty-five degrees. As we drew closer to the shore, I could hear through the water the pounding of the surf and feel the push and pull from the force of the waves overhead. I backed off on the scooter throttle when I could no longer maintain a depth of ten feet without hitting the sea floor. Before long, the surf was breaking right over our heads. I let the scooter work through the foam until the water was knee-high and we had to stand.

I removed my fins and struggled with my heavy equipment load through the surf and up to the rocky shore. When we reached the base of the cliff, I checked our location on the GPS. Then we stashed our diving gear and removed our dry suits. From inside the waterproof backpacks we retrieved our climbing gear and a set of small assault packs. Migos had the heaviest pack. He was carrying the explosives, rockets, grenades, my body armor vest and helmet. If Turki managed to escape to his panic room, we were going to have to blast him out and Migos had the kit to do it.

I wore a lightweight plastic bump helmet with a pair of mounted ANPVS-31 night vision goggles. It's hard to climb with goggles because of how they distort depth perception. I locked them in the stow position, as I wasn't going to need them to find a line up the ninety-five-foot cliff in this light. I clipped the end of the one-hundred-fifty-foot rope to the climbing harness around my waist and began the ascent.

The sandstone cliff was perfectly vertical. On the rock climber's scale, it was going to be a 5.9 most of the way, with pretty easy hand and foot holds. On the last twenty feet, the ledge extends beyond the face of the cliff and the level of difficulty goes way up, at least a 5.11, even 5.12. I made steady progress on the first pitch. On the way up, every fifteen feet or so, I emplaced a friend, which is a spring-loaded camming device. Emplacing protection is pretty simple; I would place a friend into a crack in the wall, release it to open the cam, lock it in, and then slip the rope into the carabiner pre-attached to the end of the friend.

It took me only twenty-five minutes to make it up the first seventy-five feet. When I reached the overhang, what little light I had from the moon disappeared. I paused, flipped down my night vision, and studied the contours of the overhang above me. I depressed the push-to-talk switch on my radio.

"This might get a little loud. How's it looking above me, Mac?" I asked McDonald, who was watching the objective through the infra-red payload of a VBAT UAV he was orbiting three thousand feet above the estate.

"It's clear, no security in the back yard or porch," McDonald said.

"All right Migos, get ready," I said through my throat microphone.

"On belay," he replied.

I had six friends attached to my climbing harness that, instead of a carabiner connected to the attaching wire, had a six-inch loop of one-inch nylon tubing. I took the first one, reached as high as I could, and secured it above me. With my left hand, I grabbed the nylon loop I had just installed and swung out from the cliff face one-handed. At the end of my swing, I stuck the second friend into a crack with my right hand. As I began to swing back like a pendulum, I dropped my right hand into the loop of nylon. I was now hanging by both arms. I let go with my left hand and retrieved a third friend. Hanging with just my right arm, I started to kick and began to swing. With the momentum of my body going forward, I reached out with my left and stuck the friend into a waiting crack. Once again, I was hanging from both arms.

My arms were trembling from the strain and my hands were burning from the straps. I only needed to create one more hand-hold to reach the edge. I let go of a loop with my right hand and reached down to retrieve another friend. My left arm was burning and then it wasn't. I could picture in my mind the rock crumbling around the friend that was securing my left hand as I dropped from the overhang into the dark space below. I fell twenty feet, and then the rope attached to my climbing harness around my waist arrested my fall. Before I could register the pain in my groin, I swung into the cliff face and smacked hard against the wall. My helmet made a loud crack as it bounced off the rocky cliff face. I spun my body and turned toward the cliff face, my hands searching feverishly for something to hold. Once stable, I found toeholds to support my weight.

"Are you good?" I heard Migos say.

"Yeah, I almost made it. Give me a second," I said as I straddled the climbing rope that led up to where I had emplaced my last protection.

"Climbing," I said.

"On belay," Migos replied. It was an easy climb back up to the dreaded overhang.

"Give me some slack," I said to Migos.

"Wilco," he replied.

I retrieved a friend from my harness and looped the nylon around my right wrist. I grabbed the first handhold I had emplaced on the overhand with my left hand and I swung outward like a monkey and grabbed the second with my right hand. I let go with my left hand and kept the momentum going and grabbed the last loop with my left hand. I let go with my right and I dropped my arm to let the friend looped around my wrist fall into my right hand. At the limit of my forward movement, I stabbed the friend into the waiting crack and held on. Once again, I was hanging from both hands beneath the horizontal rock overhang. I let go with my left hand. This time the protection held. Once I stopped swinging, I reached down to my harness and retrieved a carabiner with a four-foot loop of nylon webbing attached. With my left hand, I attached the carabiner to the attaching wire of the same friend attached to the loop in the right hand. My arms began to tremble, and my hands were starting to burn from holding up my weight.

I looked down and brought my right knee up and threaded my foot into the long nylon loop. Then I extended my leg and took all of the pressure off my rapidly failing arms. I was at the edge of the overhang. Now I just had to get myself over it. I emplaced another friend and, with another long loop of nylon, made another foothold. I secured the last foothold at the very edge of the overhang. I put my left foot into the new loop. I stepped out of my right foothold and rotated my body, so I was facing the cliff. I placed both hands on the edge of the cliff and pulled myself up by my arms. When my chest hit the cliff, I swung my right leg over the edge and rolled myself over the top. I rolled over onto my back at the top of the cliff.

"I made it," I said into the radio.

"About time," Migos said.

"I cheated so bad, the entire mountaineering world is bowing its collective head in shame."

"I'm coming up. We'll deduct your style points later," Migos said.

"Give me a minute to secure the rope." I tied the rope to the small safety fence Turki had placed at the edge of his lawn to keep people from wandering off the edge of the cliff.

"All clear," McDonald said.

"On belay," I said. Migos came up fast, with the aid of a pair of jumar ascenders that effectively turn the rope into a ladder. He retrieved the protection I had emplaced on the way up. When he was finished and standing next to me on the cliff top, the rope hung straight down from the overhang. This was important to us, because rappelling down that rope was part of our exit plan.

Migos dropped his heavy pack and we divided up the gear. After I drank a liter of water and ate a power bar, I took the body armor and helmet he carried for me in the pack and put it on. In addition to stopping bullets, the vest had six magazines of spare ammunition for my suppressed M4 and six M67 frag grenades in the pouches.

We approached the house from the back. The back yard was a football field. It was a hundred yards of flat open lawn, without even a single tree to hide behind. It was two in the morning, and except for Turki's security, we didn't expect anyone to be awake.

The house was an imposing, two-story structure with a main structure and two smaller wings. It was made of grey stone and had several balconies. We were bypassing the swimming pool in the back when the backyard lights went on. I dropped to the prone and flipped up my NVGs as the firing started. We were both exposed on the open lawn. I laid down a base of fire aimed at the first-floor window where the first burst of fire came from. Migos sprinted the final fifty feet to the outer wall of the house. Once at the house, he moved to the offending window and tossed in a grenade.

I ran to him after the grenade exploded. He followed me as I passed him and dove through the damaged window. Most of the lights had been turned on in the house. We entered a hallway in the west wing. Migos shot a guard trying to engage us as we made our way to the main entry. When we reached the entry, two guards fired down at us from the second-floor balcony overlooking the hall. We retreated to find a second set of stairs leading up to the second floor. We reached the end of the first-floor west wing hallway. I opened the door at the end of the hall and looked in. It was a garage. On one of the walls, I saw a fuse box. I killed the power to the house. We both dropped our NVGs and returned to the hallway.

We found a second set of stairs off the kitchen. I led the way up. These were narrow servants' stairs, and when I tried to exit into the second-floor west wing hallway, bullets pounded against the wall, inches above my head. I rolled a grenade toward the firer and dropped back down the stairs. The frag grenade created an enormous explosion inside the confined hallway. As soon as it detonated, I sprang out, with Migos close behind. I shot one of the guards who had engaged us earlier from the balcony area overlooking the main hallway. We advanced to that same balcony area. Fire from two directions caused the both of us to drop flat to the prone position. Three hallways jutted off from the main hallway; we had cleared one hallway and were receiving fire from the other two.

"Which way?" Migos asked.

"Turki will be down that hallway." I pointed to the one that led down the east wing of the house.

"We need to clear the other hallway before we can go down there," he said.

"This staircase is the nexus for the whole house. We need you to stay here to control it." As I said that, automatic fire rang out from one of the rooms at the end of the north hallway.

"Give me one of those LAWs," I said.

"It's too close."

"Just go down the stairs a little." Migos was lying prone next to the stairs; he slid down to the first landing. I extended the thermobaric rocket launcher and stuck it into the north-facing hallway that was perpendicular to the main hallway from where we were receiving the fire. Bullets ricocheted all around us, and muzzle flashes from the hallway were a nonstop light show. I pulled out the safety and fired the LAW down the narrow hallway in the general direction of the room where most of the fire was coming from. A huge explosion followed. Most of my body was behind the wall leading into the hallway, but I felt the wave of heat sweep past me as I ducked behind the wall. I picked up my rifle and headed down the east wing corridor to find Turki.

The first room I entered was empty. It was a bedroom. I was wearing my night vision, and the laser from my rifle crisscrossed the room in a searching pattern. I went back into the hallway, and with my back against the wall, reached over to open the door to the next room in the hallway. Bullets blasted through the partially open wooden door. After I pulled the pin, I let go of the spoon of the grenade in my hand, counted to three and then tossed it through the door gap into the room behind.

The blast shook the house. I continued my advance down the hallway. I went to the next room and then the next and the next. I used up all of my grenades before reaching the end of the corridor.

"Any movement on your end?" I asked Migos.

"I took care of it. I think all of the guards in this house are dead," he replied.

The house was on fire. The wing of the house where I had launched the LAW was burning, and the smoke was making it difficult to breathe and to see.

"Come to me. It's time to search those rooms I fragged," I said.

Migos and I entered each of the rooms off the hallway. We found dead guards in some of them, but no sign of Turki. The last room in the hallway, the room on the backside of the house, overlooking the lawn and the Strait of Gibraltar, was obviously the master bedroom. Two guards were in the main bedroom area and had been felled by the blast from my grenade. There was no sign of Turki.

The room was enormous; it was connected to two large bath-rooms and two walk-in closets.

"I'll bet his panic room is connected to one of these closets," Migos said.

"McDonald, how much time do we have?" I asked.

"No reaction from police or fire. You have lots of time."

We checked both walk-in closets and didn't find anything. I ran downstairs and turned the power back on. With the lights on, we saw things we missed with our night vision. Inside the linen closet in one of the bathrooms, Migos found a panel that opened into a narrow hallway. He pointed it out to me and I followed behind, down through a short hallway until it ended at a metal door. The door had to be the entrance to a panic room.

"We're going to need one of those steel-cutting shape charges," I said. It was getting smokier in the hallway, as the fire in the west wing was growing. Migos went into his pack and retrieved a five-kilo shape charge. The explosive was shaped like a cone and was in a plastic mold that allowed it to be attached with the pointy side aimed at the wall.

Migos started to tape the device to the metal door. There was a camera above the door, so I knew Turki knew what we were doing.

"Don't do that," came a voice from an unseen speaker.

"Don't do what?" Migos replied.

"Whatever you're doing. Let's talk, we can reach an agreement," the speaker said.

"Sorry, once you ordered the murder of my guys, the time for agreements ended. Don't worry, the blast will kill you instantly; you won't even feel the pain from the fire," I said.

"We're coming out. Stop. We're coming out. We surrender. Stop," the speaker said, in a panicked voice.

The hallway we were inside was cramped. Migos and I both backed out of the hallway and into the bathroom. We heard the metallic sounds of the door unlocking and a whoosh of air from an overpressure system when the panic room door unsealed. The first person we saw was a girl. She was a black girl wearing pajamas. Her eyes were wide with terror. We couldn't see anyone behind her.

"Drop to your knees and then lie flat on the floor," I said. The girl didn't move.

"Drop and lay flat or we'll shoot," I said. Still, she continued to slowly creep towards us. Migos and I readied our weapons. Suddenly the girl bolted forward. Migos and I both fired. The girl dropped in the hallway before she could reach us. Then there was an explosion. I was blown backward onto the tile floors next to the bathtub. Dust and smoke filled the room. Gunfire erupted from the hallway behind the closet. I sat up and fired into the closet. I heard Migos engage from his position on the bathroom floor. I sprang up and rushed back into the closet and the hallway behind. I stepped over the badly blown up girl and shot a guard kneeling behind her. He was wounded and trying to reload his MP-5 with only one good arm. I noticed the panic room door was closing. I stuck the barrel of my rifle between the heavy metal door and the frame, just before it fully closed. I let go of the stuck weapon and stuck my fingers into the narrow gap, prying the door open with both hands.

I had the door almost all the way open when my chest exploded with pain. I fell straight back onto the dead guard in the hallway. A mad minute of gunfire erupted above me and then ended abruptly. I could barely breathe. I heard dragging behind me. Migos grabbed me by the handle on the collar of my body armor vest and dragged me out of the narrow hallway and into the bathroom.

"Are you ok?"

"It hit the plate," I said in a raspy voice.

Migos walked past me and went back into the hallway. A few seconds later I heard the distinct sound of a suppressed M4. Migos emptied a full magazine in rapid fire. I was up onto my knees by the time he emerged from the hallway.

"We better get out of here," I said.

"Lead the way, boss."

We rappelled down the cliff. Migos went first. Before I stepped off, I looked at the house one last time. Smoke was billowing out of the upper floor windows. I let the rope play through my right hand and the figure-eight attached to my harness and abseiled to the water's edge below.

We put our dive gear back on and headed back to the yacht. I stayed barely below the surface for most of the route. After thirty minutes, I broke the surface and looked for the yacht. It took another ten minutes of skimming before we reached the boat. McDonald had to drag both of us onto the ramp. I was exhausted. My ribs were bruised, and even the salt water couldn't rinse the taste of smoke from my mouth.

I showered and went upstairs to the salon. The yacht was underway. McDonald was in the wheelhouse and had us on course for Paphos. Migos handed me a cold bottle of Sam Adams.

"Here's to Jankowski and Burnia," he said.

"Let's not forget Patton and Dornan."

We clinked bottles.

"Feel like getting drunk?" he asked.

"Yeah, as a matter of fact, I do."

CHAPTER 37

Washington DC

I watched as the maître d' at the Capital Grill escorted Cheryl and Mike to my table. I was seated at one of the big round tables in the far corner. I stood and gave Cheryl a hug and then Mike. The waiter came over and poured both of them a glass from the bottle of wine that was already on the table. I ordered a few appetizers and told the waiter we were going to talk a while before ordering dinner. The expensive Bordeaux must've bought some goodwill, because he didn't seem concerned about my plans to ruin a quick turnover of the table.

"Everything go OK in Morocco?" Mike asked.

"Mission accomplished. A bit messy, but we got the job done."

"A couple of A-list assaulters would've come in handy on a job like that."

"You won't get any arguments from Migos or me on that. There were no style points earned on that one."

"I saw the post-op satellite imagery. You would've done less damage if you shelled the place with a battleship."

"It wasn't surgical, but we didn't have great intel and we were understaffed."

"Did you at least interview some of the people on that list of names I sent you?"

"I did; I picked two. They start next month."

"Who did you pick?"

"Savage and Sorenson, same profile as before."

"Both from the Unit?"

"Yes, good guys, they'll fit in. When do I get my woman back?"

"Soon, she's almost done. Everybody loves her at the Company. My boss doesn't want her to leave."

"Tell the Director that if I don't get my girl back, I'm going to unleash Evan Moskowitz on him."

"We approached Evan; he says he'll only talk with you."

"We've bonded; who can blame him?"

"You need to wean him away from that."

"I'll try. Working with him isn't exactly my dream job."

"I'll report that upstairs. It might help get your shopping list approved."

"I give you ALICE, David Forrest, and Cheryl for way too long. I offer you Evan Moskowitz on a silver platter, and all I ask in return is to replace a few items of equipment. So far, the only answer I've received is crickets."

"Ninety-two million is a lot of money."

"It's not my equipment. I just borrow it to use in the service of God and Country."

"I'll try that line tomorrow."

"I would appreciate it. The hangar and offices will be finished next month. Now I need my toys replaced."

"And you can't do it yourself?"

"I have a short, angry office manager at Trident headquarters who won't let me."

"Maybe it's time to stop with the expensive wines, cut back, tighten the belt, downsize the yacht, live like a normal person."

"That's not practical, my lifestyle is part of my cover. It's a spy thing. Besides, I paid to rebuild Clearwater; it's only fair the Agency pays its share to rebuild Trident."

"I'll get it done somehow."

"Thanks. I would think the leadership would be throwing money at you. When gas was at six bucks a gallon there was no way the guy in the White House was going to get re-elected, now at least he has a shot. He should show some love."

"Things are calming down. That's for certain."

"Did you get the credit or did some political infighter steal your glory?"

"I got some of the credit—also some of the blame. Not everyone is happy Evan Moskowitz is still converting oxygen to carbon dioxide."

"Let me know, and I'll have Evan do a deep dive into whoever it is. He must have something to hide if he's so threatened by him."

"Probably not a good idea to run a background on the Director of National Intelligence."

"I'll hold off for now, but just say the word and we'll proceed. Evan is like a puppy who's desperate to please."

We finished the appetizers and ordered steaks. Mike left, and Cheryl and I stayed for coffee.

"You've been awfully quiet," I said.

"You and Mike had some ground you had to cover. I didn't want to interfere."

"You're never interfering. Are you ready to leave this town?"

"I can't wait. I'm excited about what we've accomplished, but I missed you."

"I'm glad to hear you say that; I was getting jealous of David Forrest."

"He's a great guy. You may have reason to worry."

"He named his computer; that should be a disqualifier right there."

"Let's go. I think I know how to cure your jealousy," Cheryl said while reaching under the table.

"Check, please!"

Dear Reader, thank you for reading Arabian Deception.
If you are interested in receiving an email notification of future releases
of Pat Walsh's adventures, use the link below:

https://landing.mailerlite.com/webforms/landing/r4u2m3

Other books by James Lawrence

Arabian Deception
Arabian Vengeance
Arabian Fury

TURN THE PAGE FOR A STUNNING PREVIEW OF

ARABIAN
DECEPTION

THE FIRST NOVEL IN THE ARABIAN ADVENTURE
SERIES BY JAMES LAWRENCE

Chapter 1

Washington, D.C.

Pat pulled into a parking space at the Pentagon in his '98 Ford Windstar minivan and began the trek across the icy asphalt to the building entrance. It was still dark, almost dawn on a late winter morning, and his face and hands were stinging from the cold. It had been ninety-two degrees when he had left Baghdad the previous week, and it was going to take some time to adjust this weather.

Pat was on a one-year assignment at the Pentagon, prepositioned for his class date next year at the National War College. He regretted never buying an overcoat for his Class A uniform; the green polyester suit was useless against the wind and cold. The work he did in the military rarely required dress uniforms, and it had just never made sense to spend money he didn't have on the accessories. By the time he stepped into the entryway and passed through security, his fingers were so frozen, he had trouble removing his access badge from his pocket.

He managed to find his office without having to ask anyone for directions, a big improvement from his first few days on the job, which had occurred last week. Pat shared an office with two other colonels and a major. Officially, they all had grand titles, but when he had first arrived and asked his office mates what they did, they'd all chimed in unison, "Slide monkeys for the chief." Pat's orders to the Pentagon had assigned him to the Army Special Operations Cell within the Army's G3 shop, but when he had shown up, he had been redirected to the Army Chief of Staff's Office and placed in a small windowless office with the other "Slide Monkeys."

Their four desks are all crammed together, facing each other bullpen style, where they all could see each other over their computer monitors. Pat could feel the attention of the other three guys as he removed his uniform jacket and hung it up on the stand behind his seat. The chief's inner circle consisted of a group of hand-selected officers from his previous commands. The chief was a tanker, an armor officer, and those commands were all armor and cavalry units. As an infantry officer with a Special Operations background, Pat was the oddball of the group.

Colonel Chris Mattingly was the senior officer in charge of their little section. He was an outgoing, friendly guy. He had worked with the chief off and on for the past twenty years. On Pat's first day, Pat had asked him how he'd wound up getting transferred.

"The guys at infantry branch told me the prepo to D.C. was a reward from a grateful nation. Working as a slide monkey in a dungeon didn't seem like much of a reward," Pat had said.

After spending the previous year in Iraq as a JSOTF commander and the two years before that in Afghanistan as the commander of a Tier 1 special mission unit, Pat felt like he deserved some downtime to get reacquainted with his family. Pat's wife was barely talking to him, and his youngest hadn't recognized him the last time he'd come home on leave. Instead, Pat wound up in a job where he was spending two hours a day commuting in D.C. traffic on top of the fourteen hours a day he spent making PowerPoint slides and attending briefings.

"Pat, you've been brought into our little section because you're a snake eater. And the SecDef has a special fondness for snake eaters. The SecDef's Green Berets conquered Afghanistan on horseback and you, the hero, Colonel Pat Walsh, personally captured Saddam Hussein. The boss brought you here to be the horse whisperer to the SecDef. The man is infatuated with Green Berets, Delta, SEALs, Rangers and all that Special Operations ninja stuff that's not worth a damn in a real war, and the chief thinks you're going to be the magic microphone he needs to get his message through to his boss."

Pat just shrugged his shoulders. It seemed pretty stupid, but it wasn't his fight. He just figured he'd roll with it and mark his time until his class started at the National War College.

Now on his second week, resigned to his role, Pat slid into his workstation.

"What do you need me to do?" Pat asked Chris after he sat down.

"Review this slide presentation. You're going to brief sometime today, whenever the boss gets in to see the SecDef," said Chris.

"I'm going to brief Secretary Rumsfeld?" Pat asked.

"Yeah, the chief will back you up. Is that a problem?"

"No, not really."

"What's the highest level you've ever briefed?" asked Chris, sensing Pat's anxiety.

"POTUS," Pat said.

"Which one?"

"All of them, since Reagan."

"Really?"

"We get a lot of oversight on my side of the business," Pat said.

"This should be a walk in the park for you. Familiarize yourself with the presentation and be ready to brief when called," Chris said.

For the first time, Pat noticed the fatigue on Chris and the rest of the team. "Have you guys been up all night putting this briefing together?" he asked.

"Yeah," Chris said.

"You should've told me. I would've stayed."

"It's okay, we needed you to be fresh this morning," said Chris.

Pat spent the next two hours going through the briefing, rehearsing his lines, which were written below in the notes section.

"You're on. The chief is waiting for you," said Chris.

Pat put his jacket back on and Chris grabbed a laptop and walked with him into the Army chief of staff's waiting room. Chris breezed by the secretary with a nod and led him into the office.

The general was a small but imposing figure. Pat had never met him before, but he had read a lot about him. He'd lost half of his left foot in Vietnam and was highly regarded as a deep thinker and a futurist. They shook hands.

"Are you getting settled?" he asked.

"Yes, sir. The family is moved in and the kids are already in school."

"Where are you living?"

"Woodbridge."

"How's the commute?"

"It's between one and two hours depending on the traffic."

"D.C. traffic is enough to make you miss Iraq," he said.

"It's good to be back."

"What are your thoughts on the brief?"

"Makes sense to me," Pat said.

He chuckled. "Let's get moving."

They filed out of the office by seniority, the chief in the lead and Pat in the back. They wound through a maze of hallways for a while and then took a private corridor into the SecDef's office suite. The conference room furnishings consisted only of a single rectangle table with six seats around it. Chris connected the laptop to the AV system. Minutes later, the SecDef and two of his assistants came in. Chris and Pat popped to attention. The SecDef didn't greet either of them. He took a seat at the head of the table and acknowledged the chief with a nod. Two assistants in civilian attire sat on his right. Neither introduced themselves. The chief and Chris sat on his left. Pat stood at the end of the table next to the screen and waiting for his cue to start talking.

The SecDef stared at Pat for what felt like minutes. It was an uncomfortable silence, and Pat looked to the chief for a signal.

"Sir, today we would like to brief you on some analysis and recommendations for your consideration regarding future troop levels in Iraq," the chief interjected.

"Has Dick Myers seen this?" asked the SecDef, referring to the chairman of the Joint Chiefs of Staff.

"No, sir," replied the chief.

The SecDef was silent and went back to staring at Pat some more. He was an older gentleman, with silver-gray hair and steel-rimmed glasses. He and Pat were ten feet apart, and Pat could feel him studying the details of his uniform.

"How long have you been in the service, Colonel?" he asked.

"Twenty years," Pat replied.

His eyes went from Pat's uniform to those of Chris and the chief.

"Why do these two other officers have eight rows of ribbons and a bunch of badges, and you only have only one row and only two badges?"

"I choose not to wear everything I'm authorized, sir."

"Why?"

"The ones I don't wear are just participation awards, and when I wear a lot of badges and medals on my uniform, it makes me feel like a South American dictator," Pat replied.

"I can't see from here. Tell me about the ones that have meaning to you."

"Purple Heart with three oak leaf clusters, Bronze Star with V device and four oak leaf clusters, Silver Star with oak leaf cluster and Distinguished Service Cross," Pat replied.

The SecDef went back to staring at him for another minute and then he took out a mechanical pencil from his pocket and made some notes on the notepad in front of him. Finally, he looked up.

"Begin," he said.

"Sir, this briefing is classified top secret. The subject of this briefing is the proposed force levels for Operation Enduring Freedom..." For the next forty-five minutes, Pat went through the slides and briefed the Army chief of staff's recommendation for increasing the force levels in Iraq. The SecDef and his staffers didn't ask any questions, but occasionally the chief would cut in on him and provide additional information and insights. The logic behind the argument was straightforward. Basically, it was a historical comparison of US Peacekeeping missions and the ratios between US troops and the occupied populations. The conclusion of the briefing was that the people of Iraq were no less hostile than the people of Kosovo and that if they used the same ratios that had been required to pacify the population of Kosovo, in Iraq, it would require a minimum of four hundred thousand additional troops.

"Sir, this completes the briefing, subject to your questions," Pat said as he grabbed for the bottle of water on the table in front of him.

"You realize that this subject has already been reviewed and a decision has been made by the National Command Authority," the SecDef said to the chief.

"Yes, sir, I do, However, I felt compelled to provide you this information, because I don't think the historical context has ever been fully considered," replied the chief.

The SecDef started tapping his heavy mechanical pencil against the table. Then he turned to Pat. As if noticing the name tag on my uniform for the first time, he said, "What about you, Walsh? What do you think?"

"Sir, I was in Iraq from the invasion in March 2003 until last week. At first, we were welcomed as liberators, but over the past year, the situation has grown increasingly hostile. The population is turning against us. I think you either have to go big or you have to get out, because right now, we seem to have enough people on the ground to provide our enemy plenty of soft targets of opportunity, but we don't have sufficient forces to suppress the threat sufficiently to prevent those attacks," Pat said.

"Suppress the threat—what does that even mean?"

"It means to neutralize through show of force. Excluding the crazy suicidal people, who are rare, if people know they're guaranteed to die if they rise up, as a general rule, they don't rise up. Showing force reduces attacks," Pat replied.

"What did you do in Iraq?" asked the SecDef.

"I commanded a Joint Special Operations Task Force responsible for the prosecution of high-value targets," Pat replied.

"And how's that going?"

"We've taken out almost the entire deck of cards from Saddam Hussein, the Ace of Spades, all the way down to the Two of Clubs, and yet the security situation isn't improving."

The SecDef returned his attention to the chief. He started out politely in a Yankee patrician dialect, the kind Pat imagined you got from one of those elite boarding schools in New England. In a scholarly and at times slightly sarcastic manner, he rebutted point by point every element contained in the briefing. He took pains to ridicule Pat's comment on "suppressing the threat" by explaining that you didn't need people in the modern era to accomplish that task. He explained that all you needed was the effective employment of technology and Special Forces. A couple of times the chief tried to respond, but the SecDef cut him off each time with a hand gesture. Pat started to lose focus when he realized that it wasn't a conversation, it was a reprimand. At the end, the SecDef launched into a tangent on "known knowns," "known unknowns," and "unknown unknowns," followed by an explanation of military tactics that was completely foreign to anything Pat had ever been taught, so Pat just stood at a rigid position of parade rest and watched as the SecDef became more and more condescending, sarcastic, insulting and abusive to Pat's boss. After a twenty-minute berating, the SecDef and his two minions got up and walked out, leaving the three of them at the table.

The chief's face was ashen. He was Asian American, and the difference from his normal coloring was stark. Chris loudly packed up his laptop, his jaws clenched and his eyes bulging with fury.

"You know the only military experience that guy has is two years as a pilot in the Navy in the 1950s," said Chris.

"I don't want to hear any of that. We need to get back. I have other things on my schedule," the chief replied.

Made in the USA
Lexington, KY
06 September 2019